APP-ILY EVER AFTER

ALSO BY J.L. JARVIS

Drake & Wilde Mysteries

Love in the Time of Pumpkins
Secrets in the Hollow
Shadow of the Horseman

Standalones

A Kiss in the Rain
App-ily Ever After
Once Upon a Winter
The Red Rose
Highland Vow

Short Stories

Seasons of Love: A Short Story Collection
The Eleventh-Hour Pact
A Christmas Yarn
The Farmer and the Belle
Work-Crush Balance

Cedar Creek

Christmas at Cedar Creek
Snowstorm at Cedar Creek
Sunlight on Cedar Creek

Pine Harbor

Allison's Pine Harbor Summer

Evelyn's Pine Harbor Autumn
Lydia's Pine Harbor Christmas

Holiday House
The Christmas Cabin
The Winter Lodge
The Lighthouse
The Christmas Castle
The Beach House
The Christmas Tree Inn
The Holiday Hideaway

Highland Passage
Highland Passage
Knight Errant
Lost Bride

Highland Soldiers
The Enemy
The Betrayal
The Return
The Wanderer

American Hearts
Secret Hearts
Forbidden Hearts
Runaway Hearts

For more information, visit jljarvis.com.

Get monthly book news at news.jljarvis.com.

APP-ILY EVER AFTER

A WORKPLACE ROMANCE

J.L. JARVIS

BOOKBINDER PRESS

GET THE AUDIOBOOK

jljarvis.com/appily/

APP-ILY EVER AFTER

Copyright © 2025 J.L. Jarvis

Published by Bookbinder Press
bookbinderpress.com

ISBN (ebook) 978-1-942767-79-4
ISBN (paperback) 978-1-942767-80-0

S carlett Rees rushed through the office corridor past a maze of cubicles, her heels clicking against the floor tiles. She glanced at her watch and muttered under her breath, "Five minutes late and counting." Her director had invited her to this meeting to consult on the development of a new app. Her presence was, she presumed, an afterthought prompted by a hallway conversation with Max—short for Maxine—Pembroke, director of research and development. Their brief chat was cut short by Max's administrator, who whisked her away for something far more important than Scarlett. Max turned back and said, "I'll catch you up on the details later." Later never quite came, but Scarlett had no worries. She knew they'd touch base at some point after the meeting—if she ever made it there.

From the start, her morning had been peppered with frustrating events—beginning with a near collision when a car with no brake lights cut her off, jostling her coffee cup and leaving splashes of Italian roast down the front of her favorite silk blouse. Then, a rogue family of ducks crossed the road to the village park's charming little pond. After cursing at the fluffy, feathered creatures and feeling a pang of guilt for having done so, she drove on toward the parking lot. Once there, she sighed with relief—until she discovered the last parking space had been taken. Now desperate, she headed for the forbidden visitor spaces, but every last one was occupied. Her final resort was the side of the road, a good half mile's walk away.

Once she sank her heels into the grassy shoulder, she slung her valise over her shoulder and grumbled, "Oh well. What's another five minutes when you're already late?"

In heels, the jog would have been long, but she tripped on the way, landed on all fours, and scraped her knee through what had become her torn pants. Propelled onward by a few choice words for the person who stole her parking spot, she pulled off her heels and hobbled barefoot the rest of the way to the building.

Scarlett prided herself on punctuality, which made being late all the more irritating. As she hurried through the corridor, she caught her reflection in the glass walls —her copper hair falling from its usually pristine bun, her favorite silk blouse now sporting an impressive coffee constellation. At thirty-two, she'd hoped to have her life more together than this. Her time at art school had taught her to see beauty in imperfection, but that appreciation rarely extended to herself. She had traded her dreams of gallery openings for a steadier paycheck from UI design, telling herself it was just temporary.

Five years later, "temporary" had become her new normal. Still, she couldn't quite squash that creative spark that made her see the world differently—both a blessing and a curse in the corporate tech world.

With a rehearsed apology at the ready, she burst into the conference room. Her words caught in her throat as she took in the scene before her. The conference table was not only packed with the usual suspects —developers, project managers, and her director—but also with two VPs, people she usually saw from a distance who took little notice of lowly corporate serfs like her. The clearing of someone's throat drew Scarlet's attention to a person at the front of the room—a tall, chestnut-haired man whose piercing eyes now bore through hers. With an apologetic smile that he didn't return, Scarlett slid into a chair at the opposite end of the conference table.

He was clearly in the middle of a presentation—or had been before she barged in. All eyes fixed on her for a moment then darted away with barely concealed condescension. He blinked and continued, his voice clipped and businesslike. "Our AI-powered app will bring entire lives—well, to life—but in a fresh, social media-rich iteration. In short, this will revolutionize the self-discovery market."

Scarlett couldn't help but raise an eyebrow at his robotic enthusiasm. For a tech nerd, he could do a decent hard sell, complete with strong, animated gestures.

And nice shoulders and arms. He didn't get those muscles from hammering code on a keyboard.

His athletic build notwithstanding, she'd heard this sort of pitch so many times—just another tech bro promising to change the world with a gimmicky app.

Scarlett cleared her own throat, once more interrupting his monologue. "Sorry again for being late, but um... question: how exactly is this app going to 'revolutionize' the self-absorbed market?"

"The self-discovery market," he corrected with an icy stare.

Ignoring his overreaction to her guileless question, she pressed on. "I guess what I'm asking is: isn't this just another journaling app for screen addicts?"

When he, too, raised an eyebrow, his face an impassive mask, Scarlett took it as her cue to back off. She'd come to realize early on in her career that the workplace had two types of people: those who were driven by curiosity and those who hated the first type. No question which type he was. Her eyes darted about to the others, who all seemed to regard her as they might a zoo exhibit, only with less interest. Scarlett tried to backpedal. "By which I mean self-reflection is good."

The man paused, his jaw tightening almost imperceptibly. "Actually," he said, his voice calm but chilling, "ChronicleMe is much more than... that."

Scarlett tried not to wince at the fleeting pain in his eyes. Now weighed down by guilt, she averted her gaze, but wherever she looked, everyone was staring at her. She stammered. "Uh, I'm sure it is." Then she froze, mouth agape, drawing a blank on his name. She'd seen him around and sat in meetings with him. She was nearly sure they'd even been introduced. For months, he'd been sitting three cubicles down—since a big corporation bought their small startup and they moved to the current glass-and-chrome building. He was one of those people scattered throughout the cubicle farm like functional fixtures. If they'd ever spoken a word to each other, she couldn't remember. But he did have a name. So what was it? *Doug? Donald? No... Dave. Yeah.* "Look, Dave—"

"Dan."

"Dan." She exhaled and then tried to look pleasant. "I just meant—" *What did I mean?* "It's a... fascinating concept—one well worth exploring."

As if unaware Scarlett was in the middle of a point, albeit an amorphous one, Max, her director, chimed in, "Absolutely!"

Scarlett's eyebrows shot up in shock, but as she recovered, she caught Max's gaze and tried to look bright-eyed.

Dan smiled warmly at Max then resumed his pitch. "ChronicleMe uses cutting-edge machine learning to analyze users' digital content and create a visually appealing timeline of their life events, milestones, and memories, along with a printable biological narrative." He continued to talk while Scarlett's mind wandered.

Blah-blah-blah... As if that charming smile will cata-pult that jumble of tech-speak past Max's keen business sense. Just surrender now, Dorothy. She's too smart for you—and your little code too! Oh God, is he still talking?

"... in effect giving ordinary people a compelling, heirloom-quality biography by a highly trained ghostwriter."

Scarlett drew in a quick—and apparently loud—breath. Which may have been more of a gasp. Heads turned. She froze, mouth gaping open again, for a moment.

Dan leveled a withering look. "Yes?"

"Oh. I was just thinking."

Dan raised an eyebrow.

Well, now that was just rude! "It could be amazing, and I'm sure there are some amazing social media posts out there, but..."

Dan stared blankly while Max's brows furrowed.

"I mean, have you looked at social media posts lately?"

It was only the look in his eyes, but Scarlett saw it as indignant. *Really? You're offended by that?*

Dan said calmly, "One or two, yes."

He did have a point. She realized he must have been buried in social media through this first phase of his project. *Oh well. Sorry?*

She tried not to laugh. "C'mon. It's all snapshots of lunch plates and, oh, look—a cat. Fluffy the Furball is licking his—" She paused, taking in the blank stares. "I mean, come on. We're not talking Annie Leibovitz, are we?"

Dan then fired a deadly shot across the bow. Silence. Total squirm-inducing silence.

Someone say something. Scarlett felt herself blush. "Sorry, but just trying to imagine a riveting narrative built around snapshots of breakfast, the top of a tour bus, or political posturing no one cares about. It ain't Shakespeare." Met with more silence, she shrugged.

"Or maybe it is. What are politics but your Montagues here and your Capulets there, all clumped together and strutting about in their codpieces?"

Blank stares. *Oh, c'mon, people. Lighten up!*

Unfazed, Dan explained as if to a child, "But that's the beauty of ChronicleMe. It has the power to be more imaginative than you." He stopped abruptly then added, "—than you might imagine."

Excuse me? Scarlett couldn't help frowning. *Did he just call me unimaginative?* Scarlett narrowed her eyes. "Well, I'd like to see that!"

Max leaned back in her chair, her eyes lit with interest. "So would I! I'm intrigued!"

After flashing a taut smile at Max, Dan cast a subtly scathing glance Scarlett's way, then went on, his voice never wavering from its professional cadence. "There's no doubt some people's lives are a light read. But imagine the implications for someone on their deathbed who wants to leave answers to questions their young child might one day have, or for an adult child seeking to understand his estranged father."

"Like genealogy research?" *Now we're making some sense.*

Dan's lips thinned into a tolerant line. "Oh, but this is so much more than dry documents, census records, or scans of crumpled papers pulled from a box in the attic. ChronicleMe's finely honed machine learning will have the power to scour a host of online resources to form a unique web—with the beauty of handcrafted lace—"

The beauty of handcrafted lace. Who's he kidding?

"—of family and friends and other online contacts. People's lives could be brought into marked relief, allowing loved ones to know them in ways they never could have before. Joyful, meaningful, or poignant moments in life could be remembered and passed down, preserving their digital legacy for future generations."

Wow, did he ever miss his calling? He could open a word-salad bar.

My app, blah-blah-blah... He's passionate—about his ideas, anyway. Elsewhere remains to be seen. She tried not to smirk as she inwardly chuckled. But in that instant, as if reading her thoughts, he shot her a look—a burning, unsettling look. Scarlett's heart skipped a beat. Her eyes locked with his for a moment. Scarlett told herself the fire in his eyes was merely left over from describing the project he loved.

His eyes darted away, and the moment ended. Scarlett could breathe. But now she wondered.

"I love it!" Her boss, Max, the emotionless director of research and development, practically had tears in her eyes as she said that.

Scarlett watched her, amazed. Had they been in the same meeting? Had they heard the same pitch? More importantly, had she ever seen Max so enthused? About anything? Scarlett realized she was shaking her head. After suddenly stopping, she glanced around. No one noticed. No, wait. Dan did. In one instant of eye contact, he seemed to look through her with an unmistakable air of self-satisfaction.

A little sound of exasperation escaped from her

throat loudly enough for the guy sitting beside her to turn. She answered his quizzical look with a sudden fit of feigned coughing until he turned away.

When the effusive gushing over Dan's presentation finally subsided, Max closed her laptop. "Let's move forward with this. Dan, let's talk more. Schedule a spot on my calendar this week."

He replied with an eager nod.

Well, why wouldn't he be eager? His career's going great. While mine? Mine's slogging along with my state university education, which was great, except talent and skill don't really matter because I didn't get my ticket punched at a top school—like the ones I got into but couldn't afford to attend. Except, turns out, I could have because all the students who went to the fancy schools are having their college loans forgiven by the government. Meanwhile, I did the responsible thing and didn't borrow beyond my means. And look at me now. Life just isn't fair.

"Scarlett?"

She looked over at Max, who was waiting.

"I said, 'I want you to take the lead on design.'"

"Oh. Great!" *Smile. It'll look better than that deer-in-the-headlights expression that you're probably sporting. Take the lead? No one has let me take the lead since that children's-game app that no child would touch. This could bring my career back on track. Or destroy it. No pressure. But why did it have to be this project? Why me? And why him?*

Scarlett was sure every thought that she had must be written on her face, because Max seemed to answer.

"Your perspective and artistic style will complement Dan's vision."

Scarlett shot a quick look at Dan. For the first time in this meeting, his thoughts were apparent. He'd gotten a green light, and although he was now saddled with Scarlett, he'd still be in charge. An unexpected grin bloomed on his face, the sort of grin some might call winning, which Scarlett supposed he was—which meant she was losing.

And yet, if an upside existed here, this project could be an opportunity to redeem herself in Max's eyes. Scarlett would never forget the disappointment she'd seen there when the reviews came out for her last project, a children's-game app. Tax Tykes: A Double-Entry Adventure in Accounting was universally loathed by children and parents alike. In her defense, the app was never her idea. She'd merely spearheaded the artistic design. But she was part of the team, which made her part of the failure.

Scarlett smiled at Max. "Great. I'll get right on it."

"Good. Dan, why don't you get together with Scarlett sometime today and walk her through what you've got so far?"

Before Dan could reply, Max's assistant zoomed in, and the two were soon off, leaving Scarlett and Dan. Scarlett looked around at the now-empty conference room. "Wow! It's amazing how fast a room can clear out."

Dan's face remained impassive. "Yeah, well, efficiency is key in this business."

His cold response left Scarlett wrong-footed. She

attempted to lighten the mood. "Well, the pressure's off now."

His only reply was a questioning look.

Scarlett felt compelled to elaborate. "Because the project's approved." Still no response.

Dan's eyes narrowed slightly. "Yeah. Despite having my presentation disrupted by a latecomer who hadn't bothered to familiarize herself with the project."

Scarlett felt her hackles rise. "Excuse me? I was brought into this at the last minute, so I didn't have a chance. I had questions. Isn't that what meetings are for?"

"No. This particular meeting was so I could introduce my project without any disruptions."

"Oh!" she said more loudly than she'd intended. She lowered her voice. "Well, if you're so concerned about disruptions, maybe be a little more engaging so people won't notice."

A muscle twitched in Dan's jaw, the only indication that her words had any effect. "Look," he said, his voice tightly controlled, "like it or not, we're going to be working together, so I suggest we keep things professional and focus on the task at hand."

Professional? "Oh, do you? Well, I think—"

"*Everyone* knows what you think!"

"That's what I was there for—to think!"

Dan scowled. "But not to arrive late and disrupt the flow."

Scarlett cast a pitying gaze and pouted. "Oh. I disrupted your flow?"

She was ready for sarcasm, an angry retort,

anything but a cold, emotionless stare. With no warning, he turned and left.

Hold on! I wasn't finished! But he was finished— and halfway down the hall.

"Are you finished in here?" A pleasant young admin stood in the doorway. "Sorry, but we've got it signed out for the next two hours."

Scarlett turned and tried to tamp down her irritation with Dan. "Yes. Sorry. I'm leaving." Quickly, she scooped up her notes, shoved them into her valise, and was halfway to the door when the admin called out. Cord and laptop in hand, she pointed at Dan's laptop. "Don't forget your computer!"

With a glance down at her laptop clutched in her arms, Scarlett said, "Oh, it's not mine."

Judging by the admin's expression, she didn't really care.

"Never mind. I'll take care of it." Scarlett grabbed Dan's laptop and left. *Great. You had to be nice. Now you'll have to talk to him—which is why your career isn't where you think it should be, because you can't think quickly enough on your feet.*

"Scarlett, wait up," Dan called, his voice clipped as he jogged to catch up with her.

She held out his computer, trying to mask her irritation. "Here, I thought it would be more efficient if I brought this to you. Wouldn't want to disrupt another meeting's flow."

His mouth tightened at her sarcasm while an unnecessarily awkward computer handoff took place. As much as they both seemed intent on avoiding it, skin brushed against skin, sending an unexpected spark through Scarlett. *Curse you, static electricity! It's just the dry air and carpet.*

Still, Scarlett couldn't help but notice how warm his fingers felt against hers, despite his cold demeanor. She quickly dismissed the thought, chalking it up to her overactive artist's imagination—the same imagination that had once earned her accolades in art school before the realities of paying rent had steered her towards the more practical world of graphic design. Still, something about the way Dan's eyes flickered with an emotion she couldn't quite name made her wonder if there was more to this stern, infuriating man than met the eye.

Having handed off the laptop, Scarlett turned to head for her desk.

"Look," Dan said in a tone devoid of warmth.

Must I? She turned. *What now? Don't think that just because you impressed Max, I'll fall for your pitch. You and your stony face and insufferable manner.*

"We need to discuss the project parameters," Dan stated flatly.

A mix of emotions coursed through her, arriving at resignation and dread, which Dan seemed to assiduously ignore. "Now?" Scarlett asked, unable to keep the reluctance from her voice.

"Yes, now. Unless you have more important matters to attend to?" His tone made it clear he doubted that could be possible.

Scarlett paused, weighing her options. On the one hand, she'd do almost anything to avoid Dan. On the other hand, she reminded herself, this project could resurrect her floundering career. "I guess we may as well get started," she conceded.

Dan nodded curtly.

Ten minutes later, they were seated at a small table in the company cafe, steaming cups of coffee before them. She had to hand it to Dan. He commanded attention not just through his height—though Scarlett couldn't deny that at six foot two, he cut an impressive figure—but through a kind of focused intensity that seemed to radiate from him. His chestnut hair had a persistent wayward streak that defied corporate styling, and his hazel eyes held a peculiar mix of determination and hidden warmth. At thirty-five, he'd already made a name for himself in the tech world, though there were vague rumors of personal tragedy that drove him. He carried himself with the confidence of someone used to being the smartest person in the room, yet there was something almost vulnerable in the way he absently rubbed the old watch on his wrist whenever he was deep in thought.

As the silence stretched out uncomfortably, Scarlett couldn't take any more and broke it. "So," she said, her tone cautious, "ChronicleMe."

Dan leaned forward, his eyes intense but devoid of warmth. "This app will revolutionize how people understand themselves and others," he stated. "By analyzing digital footprints, we'll provide a tool for self-discovery that's both insightful and accessible."

Scarlett nodded slowly, feigning interest. *Yeah, I've already heard your pitch once today. I was there, remember?* "And how do you plan to make it user-friendly? I'm just wondering how many people will wade through your data analysis only to learn they need a hobby—besides posting pet pictures."

Dan's jaw tightened almost imperceptibly. "That's where your role comes in," he said, his tone making it clear he had doubts about her capabilities. "Max seems to think highly of your design skills."

Don't look so surprised. "I can make it look good." She said it as if she believed it. The bitter aftertaste of Tax Tykes was still on her palette.

He looked straight at her. "I want more than good. I want ChronicleMe to be so intuitive that users are barely aware of the data. It should simply flow—"

Again with the flowing. "Like a lazy river of data." *Oops. That was snarky. It just slipped out.*

His eyes narrowed. "Like the past come to life."

With renewed dedication, Scarlett strove to stay focused. "We could start with a visual timeline," she suggested, her creative mind already at work despite her dislike for the man.

Dan nodded, his face impassive. "Go on."

"We map out users' digital lives, highlighting key moments and patterns—all hyperlinked. Then we add realistic animation to key photos and interactivity with past posts."

A flicker of interest crossed his face, quickly replaced by his usual stoic expression. "Sentiment analysis could color-code different life periods, showing emotional trends."

"Like movie storyboards," Scarlett added, surprised to find common ground with him.

"Precisely." Dan paused, his eyes suddenly distant. "But ChronicleMe isn't only about preserving happy moments or creating digital scrapbooks," he said, his voice softer than Scarlett had heard before. "It's about understanding the full tapestry of a life, even the threads we might have missed or forgotten. Sometimes, those are the most important ones."

Scarlett frowned, confused by his sudden shift in tone. "What do you mean?"

But Dan had already snapped back to his businesslike demeanor. "Never mind. Let's focus on making this happen."

As they spent the next hour exchanging ideas, the project's potential began to overshadow their mutual animosity. To her surprise, Dan listened to her ideas— really listened. The more seriously he took her, the guiltier she felt about her earlier behavior. Not that he or his ideas had won her over. He was still the same aloof guy she'd sparred with in the meeting. But by the time they finished their coffee, Scarlett was surprised to find the experience hadn't been entirely unpleasant.

During their walk back to their cubicles, Dan paused at Scarlett's desk. "Thank you for sharing your... input."

Thank you for sharing? "Uh... you're welcome."

Dan's face remained impassive. "So. Back to work."

With a nearly military pivot, he turned and went back to his desk.

Bewildered by his abruptness, Scarlett watched in stunned silence as he walked away. Just as she'd begun to feel comfortable with him, he shut down any connection between them as if he'd flipped a switch. He was finished with her. She'd served her purpose, so end of discussion. Click.

As Scarlett made her way through the office, her past career failure, which was never far from her thoughts, came to mind. Just three months before, she had been the lead designer on Tax Tykes, a highly anticipated educational app for children. She had poured her heart and soul into the project, working countless late nights and weekends to perfect every detail of the interface.

But when Tax Tykes launched, it was a disaster. The app had been thoroughly tested and performed flawlessly. The graphics were gorgeous—in Scarlett's opinion, anyway. And they had a slick, multifaceted marketing scheme that was sure to succeed. Until it didn't. Children found it boring. The reviews were scathing, and within weeks, the company pulled it from app stores. While Scarlett's boss had acknowledged that the failures weren't entirely her fault, the damage to her career and confidence was done.

Now, as she settled into her desk to start work on ChronicleMe, doubt gnawed at her. She opened her design software, her cursor hovering uncertainly over the blank canvas. Tax Tykes seeped into her mind like a cloud of impending doom. What if she couldn't do this?

What if ChronicleMe turned out to be another Tax Tykes?

Scarlett shook her head, trying to shake the feeling that she was one mistake away from actualizing her dark doubts. The setback weighed on her, making her more cautious and critical—both of herself and the project—and paralyzing her creativity. How could she invest her artistic soul into another project only to see it fail? And yet she knew ChronicleMe might be her one chance at redemption. It could save her career—if she could survive working with the perplexing Dan Weston.

2

Scarlett stared at her computer screen, her fingers hovering over the keyboard as she considered the task ahead. The ChronicleMe project was officially underway, and now she was expected to transform the experience into a visually rich and riveting representation of users' social media data. How would she do that? She stared at the screen and tried to envision opening the app and embarking upon a multimedia journey of her life. There was just one problem: Scarlett's own social media presence was practically nonexistent.

In art school, she once sat in class, brush in hand, staring at a blank canvas. When her professor asked what she was thinking, she looked around at her classmates, all working away. Scarlett said, "I'm wondering what Rembrandt did when he got stuck."

Her professor smiled faintly. "I don't know. But I'll tell you what he didn't do. He didn't wonder what Leonardo da Vinci did. You don't become a great artist by being like anyone else." He glanced at the other students in class then gestured toward Scarlett and her blank canvas. "This is part of your process. Embrace it."

A BURST of laughter from the cubicle next to hers broke Scarlett's concentration. Scarlett peered over the partition and saw her colleague, Zoe Chen, giggling at something on her phone.

Looking at Zoe's cubicle was like peering into an explosion of personality. A riot of color, every surface was covered with anime figurines, motivational sticky notes written in glitter pen, and an ever-growing collection of oddly shaped stress balls. At twenty-eight, she approached both coding and life with the same boundless enthusiasm, her round face often lighting up with ideas that bounced between brilliant and bizarre. Her thick-rimmed glasses and ever-changing array of pastel hair clips couldn't quite hide the sharp intelligence behind her bubbly exterior. She had a way of disarming people with her cheerfulness while quietly solving the most complex problems on the team.

"What's so funny?" Scarlett asked, grateful for the distraction.

Zoe looked up, her round face beaming with amusement. She pushed her thick-rimmed glasses up her nose and held out her phone. "Check out this meme. Who does that remind you of?"

Scarlett leaned over and looked. The screen showed a picture of a woman in military gear climbing a wall, looking back at those struggling behind her and waving them on, saying, "There's no *I* in team!" One woman turned to another. "There's no 'us' either."

Scarlett laughed too loudly then covered her mouth. "You're going to get me into trouble."

Zoe shrugged, her colorful array of anime-themed enamel pins jingling on her lanyard. "I didn't make you laugh. That's on you."

Scarlett shook her head, smiling. Zoe was the unofficial morale booster, always ready with a smile and a quirky observation to lighten the mood.

"So," Zoe said, spinning in her chair to face Scarlett fully, "how's the ChronicleMe project going? Cracked the code to digitizing our souls yet?"

Scarlett sighed. "Not quite. I'm still trying to figure out how to transform the data analysis into art. It's... complicated."

Zoe nodded sagely. "Ah, yes. The eternal struggle of turning our messy human lives into neat little ones and zeros."

Scarlett shook her head. "That's Dan's department. I just have to make all the boring stuff pretty."

Now deep in thought, Zoe stared into the distance. "I wonder what my social media would say. Never mind. Mine would break the machine."

Scarlett's eyes lit with amusement, but her expression quickly faded. "You know... that might help."

"Breaking the machine?"

"No," Scarlett smirked. "Your social media."

Zoe perked up and asked dramatically, "You want to immortalize my digital footprint in the annals of ChronicleMe history?"

Scarlett laughed. "Not exactly. I mean, it wouldn't help Dan—at least not that I know of, but it would really help me."

Zoe's eyebrows drew together then relaxed. "Oh, I forgot! You're the only person left in the world with no social media presence."

Scarlett rolled her eyes. "Well, that's a little dramatic."

"Maybe a little—but not much." Zoe's eyes shone with warmth.

"I know it sounds weird. I'm just—"

Nodding, Zoe finished, "A private person. I know."

"But for this..." Scarlett waved her hand toward the screen with a sigh. "I just need some context. You know —normal social media stuff—like yours!"

"Hold on there. I never said it was normal." With twinkling eyes, she spun her chair back to her computer and happily rattled off her various social media handles. There was a marked contrast between the two women. While Scarlett was reserved and private, Zoe was an open book, enthusiastically sharing every aspect of her life online. She made it look so easy. It wasn't—at least for Scarlett.

"There you go," Zoe said, finishing her list. "Fair warning, there's a lot of cat pictures. And food. And cats eating food."

"Noted," Scarlett said, jotting down the information. "Thanks, Zoe. This is really helpful."

"Happy to contribute to the cause of science and/or invasive data mining," Zoe replied with a wink. "Oh, and speaking of contributing..." She rummaged in her desk drawer and pulled out a small, squishy object, which she tossed to Scarlett.

Scarlett caught it reflexively. It was a stress ball designed to look like a smiling brain. "Um, thanks?"

"For when the coding gets tough," Zoe explained. "Squeeze the brain, release the stress. It's scientifically proven. By me. Just now."

Scarlett placed the squishy brain on her desk, unable to suppress a smile. "I'll keep that in mind."

As she turned back to her computer, Scarlett felt a renewed sense of purpose. With Zoe's data as a starting point, she could begin to build a concept.

She pulled up Zoe's profiles and began to scroll through them. What she found was a whirlwind of activity—daily updates, countless photos, and check-ins at every conceivable location. The results were a refreshingly honest reflection of Zoe, in stark contrast to Scarlett's own sparse offerings.

As she began to compile a collection of screenshots and color palettes, Scarlett sensed a presence behind her. The hair on the back of her neck stood up, and she caught a whiff of a subtle, masculine scent—a mix of sandalwood and something uniquely... Dan.

"Examining social media profiles?" his deep voice rumbled close to her ear, sending an involuntary shiver down her spine. "I trust you're making efficient use of your time?"

Scarlett turned and found herself face-to-face with Dan. This close, she couldn't help but notice the flecks of gold in his hazel eyes, the strong line of his jaw, and the way his crisp white shirt stretched across his broad shoulders. She swallowed hard, annoyed at her body's traitorous response to his proximity.

"Just gathering preliminary data for context," she managed, her voice sounding steadier than she felt. "To develop a visual concept. It's a start."

Dan leaned in closer and reached past her to point at something on the screen. His arm brushed against hers, and Scarlett froze, hyperaware of every point of contact they made. As he moved the mouse, his hand accidentally grazed hers, and a jolt of electricity seemed to pass between them.

For a split second, their eyes met, and Scarlett saw a flicker of... something in Dan's gaze before his usual mask of calm professionalism slipped back into place. He cleared his throat and stepped back, putting a more respectable distance between them.

"Keep in mind," he said, his voice slightly gruffer than usual, "the more diverse the data becomes, the better our AI will be at capturing the full spectrum of human experiences."

Scarlett nodded, trying to ignore the lingering warmth where his hand had touched hers and the rapid beating of her heart. She reminded herself firmly that this man was Dan—infuriating, arrogant Dan—and any attraction was purely physical and entirely unwelcome.

She had to be suffering from some sort of corporate Stockholm Syndrome.

Still, as he turned to Zoe, she couldn't help but sneak a glance at his form, silently cursing herself for noticing how well his trousers fit him. This project would be the death of her, one way or another.

Dan said, "Zoe. I just spoke with Max. You've impressed us both with your work on the last project."

Scarlett's eyes widened. Was that praise? *I didn't know he knew how.* Zoe seemed to take his words in stride, chirping a thank-you with her usual cheery smile.

"So, it's official. You're on the ChronicleMe team."

Zoe's eyes shone. "Yay! Thanks! I can't wait to get started!"

"Stop by my desk, and I'll fill you in." With an abrupt turn to Scarlett, Dan looked down and asked, "Have you got anything of actual value yet?"

Zoe turned and, nose down, percussively typed at her keyboard.

Scarlett bristled. "Yes, just not tangible yet. We can't all derive profound insight from cat photos at first glance, but I'll keep digging."

The keyboard stopped clicking, and Zoe peeked around the cubicle wall she shared with Scarlett. "Excuse me? Have you looked at my profile? 'Cause my cat is the cutest!" She grinned.

Dan glanced her way. "Yes, Shadow."

Scarlett nearly fell out of her chair. "You've seen Shadow!"

"I make it a point to follow everyone on the team," Dan replied matter-of-factly.

Scarlett grimaced. "Why?"

His mouth twitched at the corner. "There's no 'why' in team."

Seeing Scarlett's stunned look, Dan explained, "Zoe sent me the meme."

Still puzzled, Scarlett asked Zoe, "When? I was sitting right here."

"Quick thumbs," Zoe said as she disappeared behind the cubicle wall.

Scarlett didn't realize she was frowning until she caught Dan's eye.

He explained, "Knowing one's team fosters camaraderie, which in turn fosters quality work."

Scarlett raised an eyebrow. "And you don't find that... a little invasive?" *By which I mean creepy?*

Dan gave her a puzzled look. "Isn't that the point of social media—to share? We should all be invested in the people we work with. The more we understand one another, the more successful we'll be as a team."

"But work is work, and personal lives are... not work," Scarlett countered.

Dan countered. "But social media is neither; it's data. And that's what we're tapping into with ChronicleMe—helping people see the bigger picture of their lives, the value of the connections they've made, and the ones they might be missing."

Scarlett shifted uncomfortably in her seat. "I guess. But there's a difference between voluntary sharing and having an AI dig through your personal history, making assumptions about who you are."

"Is there? Whether we're consciously sharing on social media or leaving digital footprints without realizing it, we're all putting pieces of ourselves out there. ChronicleMe is just a tool to help us make sense of it all."

Before Scarlett could respond, Zoe stacked some papers together and set them down neatly. "Ooh, are we having a philosophical debate about the nature of privacy in the digital age?" Her head popped up over the partition, her eyes sparkling with interest behind her glasses. "'Cause I have thoughts." She sighed and added. "Actually, I just need a break."

Dan looked at her with interest. "And they are…?"

"Well…" Zoe tapped her chin thoughtfully. "As the office's resident oversharer, I'm all for embracing our digital legacies. I mean, think about it—future historians will have a field day with all our tweets and Instagram posts. We're basically writing our autobiographies in real time!"

Dan unfolded his arms. "Exactly!"

Scarlett couldn't help but smile at Zoe's enthusiasm. "But don't you worry about privacy—about people misusing your information?"

Zoe shrugged. "I guess… But I figure if I'm in control of what I put out there, I'm writing my own narrative. Better that than having others define me, you know?"

Dan nodded. "And that's what ChronicleMe is all

about—giving people the tools to understand and shape their own stories."

Scarlett looked between Dan and Zoe, feeling outnumbered but not quite ready to concede the point. "I still think there's value in maintaining some privacy, in keeping parts of ourselves offline."

Dan shrugged. "We respect that, which is why we're building in robust privacy controls." Apparently seeing doubt in Scarlett's expression, Dan went on. "We're not arguing for total transparency. People can choose what to put out there, and that's different for everyone. ChronicleMe just examines what's already public."

Zoe chimed in, "Yeah, and think of the cool stuff we could discover about ourselves! Like, maybe the AI will analyze my posts and explain my obsession with purple or why my taste in men sucks." She distractedly picked up the angry-face stress ball from her cubicle shelf.

Scarlett added dryly, "Not to mention your slight addiction to collecting novelty stress balls."

Zoe set the stress ball aside. "I'll have you know my stress-ball collection is a carefully curated art installation! You, of all people, Miss Art Major, should appreciate that!"

The two women laughed while Dan stared at the squishy brain. With no warning, he straightened up. "Back to work."

As he walked away, Scarlett returned to her computer screen, leaving Zoe's colorful social media profiles still open in multiple tabs. She shook her head, trying to dispel the nagging doubts Dan had planted.

"You okay over there?" Zoe asked, her voice softer now. "You look like you're having an existential crisis. Need to squeeze the brain?"

Scarlett chuckled despite herself. "I'm fine. Just... thinking."

Zoe nodded sagely. "Dangerous pastime, that. Especially for us overthinker types." She paused then added, "You know, it's okay to be private. But it's also okay to open up a little. Maybe ChronicleMe could help you with that?"

Scarlett looked at her colleague, surprised by the insight. Sometimes, it was easy to forget that beneath Zoe's quirky exterior lay a sharp, empathetic mind. "Zoe, how do you do it?"

Zoe furrowed her eyebrows. "Do what?"

"How can you be so comfortable sharing everything online?"

Zoe's usual bubbly demeanor softened slightly, a wistful look crossing her face. "Oh. You know, it's funny. I used to be super-private, kind of like you."

Scarlett wrinkled her face. "I find that hard to imagine."

Zoe nodded, fiddling with one of her anime pins. "No, really. Back in high school, I was the quiet kid, always in the background. Nobody really knew me." She paused, her eyes distant. "Then, junior year, my dad got sick. Really sick."

Scarlett leaned in, sensing the weight of the story. "Oh, Zoe."

"He's fine now." Zoe smiled softly. "But back then, it was tough. But you know what got me through? I found this online support group for kids with sick parents. For the first time, I could share things I couldn't tell anyone else. They got me, and they helped me."

"That must have been a relief," Scarlett said gently.

"It was life-changing," Zoe agreed. "And eventually, what I was going through seemed to help others. After that, I promised myself I would always be open because you never know who might need to hear your story, you know?"

Scarlett nodded, seeing her friend in a new light. "That's... pretty amazing."

Zoe brightened, her usual perkiness returning. "I mean... those cat photos of mine could save lives!" She laughed then added, "Or make somebody smile. That's something."

"It is!" Scarlett meant it sincerely.

"And hey, if you ever want to dip your toes into the wild world of social media, I'd be happy to be your guide. We could start small. Maybe a LinkedIn profile? Or an X account where you only post about the unfathomable joy of working with me. No? How 'bout a food Instagram?"

Scarlett laughed. "I'll think about it. Thanks, Zoe."

As Zoe disappeared back into her cubicle, humming what sounded suspiciously like the theme from *The Social Network*, Scarlett turned to her computer again. She had work to do, but her mind was whirling with new thoughts and possibilities. Maybe it was time to reconsider her stance on social media. Like ChronicleMe, it was about making connections—ones you never knew you needed.

The rest of the day passed in a blur of social media pages and screenshots of Dan's project. By the time Scarlett looked up from her screen, the office was nearly empty. She stretched, feeling a satisfying pop of her spine, and began to pack up her things.

As she was shutting down her computer, a notification caught her eye. It was an invite from Dan to join a private ChronicleMe test group. The message read, "We need social media profiles for the project. I'm encouraging everyone on the team to volunteer theirs."

Scarlett wanted deeply to decline, but doing so would cast her in a negative light when she desperately needed this project to work. And, in truth, she couldn't deny her growing curiosity. Glancing at the squishy-brain stress ball then at Zoe's empty cubicle, vibrant with life even in its occupant's absence, Scarlett braced herself. With her finger poised over the mouse, she drew in a breath. *Don't overthink it.* Then she impulsively clicked Accept.

As she left the office, Scarlett had an uncomfortable feeling she'd just stepped onto a path that would change everything. But would it be for the better?

On her way out, she passed Dan's desk. He was still sitting there, bathed in the glow of his computer screen, absorbed in his work. For a moment, Scarlett felt a flicker of... something. Not admiration. Respect? Curiosity? She couldn't quite name it.

"Goodnight, Dan," Scarlett said, her tone neutral.

Dan looked up, his face impassive. "Goodnight. I'll expect a progress report first thing tomorrow."

Scarlett felt a flicker of annoyance. "Of course," she

replied, her smile not quite reaching her eyes. "See you tomorrow."

As she walked to her car, Scarlett's thoughts were on connections. People made them online, in person, and without being aware. Maybe ChronicleMe could shed light on those hidden links.

But it'll take more than an app to shed light on Dan Weston. That guy's a tech nerd disguised as a hot guy inside an enigma.

3

S carlett arrived at the office early the following day, her mind already racing with ideas for Chroni-cleMe's algorithm. As she sat down at her desk, she noticed a sticky note attached to her monitor. In Zoe's loopy handwriting, it read, "Remember, with great power comes great responsibility... and great memes. Don't forget to have fun!"

Smiling, Scarlett pinned the note to her cubicle wall and fired up her computer. She had just started reviewing yesterday's ideas when a commotion near the entrance caught her attention.

"Dan! There you are, you code-crunching Casanova!"

Scarlett looked up to see a tall, broad-shouldered guy bounding toward Dan's desk. The visitor's dark eyes sparked with mischief beneath wildly disheveled black hair, and his quick grin could charm its way past any obstacle. He was wearing a shirt that proclaimed, "I paused my game to be here," and cargo pants that seemed to have more pockets than strictly necessary.

Dan's face lit up with recognition. "Diego! What are you doing here, man?"

Diego dramatically clutched his chest. "What, I need a reason to visit my best bud? Can't a guy just drop by to bask in the glow of your Silicon Valley greatness?"

Laughing, Dan pulled Diego into a quick backslapping hug. "Seriously, though. I thought you were still in Seattle."

"Ah, well," Diego said, waving his hand dismissively, "turns out Seattle's not really my scene. Too much rain, and... they transferred me back. So I thought I'd come crash with my favorite tech genius for a while. You don't mind, right?"

Dan's expression flickered between amusement and concern. "Aw, man, you know I love you, but—"

"Great!" Diego interrupted, clapping Dan on the shoulder. "It's settled, then. Now, give me the grand tour of the new building!"

As Dan began to show Diego around the office, Scarlett couldn't help but watch them with a mix of curiosity and amusement. She had never seen Dan so... relaxed. It was a stark contrast to his usual intense focus.

Zoe's head popped up over the cubicle partition. "Lori in reception just texted there's a hottie here to see Dan," she whispered conspiratorially.

Scarlett rolled her eyes. "Yeah, some friend of his, I guess."

"Interesting..." Zoe's eyes twinkled. "Very interesting indeed."

Before Scarlett could respond, Dan and Diego rounded the corner.

Zoe's expression went blank. "Oh."

Diego's eyes locked on Zoe's.

"Scarlett," Dan said, a hint of resignation in his voice, "I'd like you to meet my former colleague and old college roommate, Diego."

Diego swept into an exaggerated bow. "Charmed, I'm sure. So, you're the brilliant minds behind ChronicleMe? Dan's told me all about it. Sounds like some real *Black Mirror* stuff, if you ask me."

Scarlett bristled slightly. "It's a tool for self-discovery and personal growth."

"Ah, a true believer!" Diego grinned. "I like it." He leaned closer and lowered his voice. "So, what deep, dark secrets has your AI uncovered?"

Dan groaned. "None. Because that's not our objective. The whole point of the app is to highlight the aspects of users' lives in a media-rich and positive way. But it's all underpinned with respect for user privacy."

Diego raised an eyebrow. "In this day and age? That's adorable."

Scarlett fought to restrain her annoyance. "Privacy is a fundamental right, not a punchline."

"Whoa, hold on," Diego said, holding up his hands in mock surrender. "I'm just messing around. But seriously, aren't you guys worried about the ethical implications of all this? I mean, giving AI access to people's entire digital lives... That's some heavy stuff."

"That's why we're being so careful with the development process," Zoe chimed in, sounding unusually serious. "We're not just throwing code at the wall and seeing what sticks. There are safeguards, protocols—"

"Where's the fun in that?" Diego interrupted. "If you're going to play God with people's data, at least make it interesting. Like, maybe the AI could predict people's future based on their past posts. Or create alternate timelines of their lives!"

Dan sighed. "Diego, that's not what ChronicleMe is about. We're trying to help people understand their lives better, not turn it into some sci-fi spectacle."

Scarlett found herself nodding. Despite her reservations about the project, she appreciated Dan's commitment to its integrity.

Diego shrugged. "Your loss. But hey, if you ever want to pivot to something more exciting, I've got tons of ideas. Like, what if—"

"Okay!" Dan interrupted, steering Diego away from the cubicles. "I think that's enough disruption for one morning. How about we grab some coffee and catch up properly?"

As they walked away, Scarlett heard Diego's animated voice fading. "Coffee? Pfft. What we need is a good old-fashioned coding bender. Remember that time in college when we stayed up for seventy-two hours straight trying to build a more user-friendly Linux distro?"

Once the two men were well out of earshot, Scarlett turned to Zoe. "Well, that was... something."

Zoe nodded, apparently still processing the whirlwind that was Diego. "Yeah, he's something, all right."

"You okay?" Scarlett asked, noticing Zoe's furrowed brow.

Zoe shook her head, trying to clear her thoughts. "Fine. It's just... Diego's not the best influence on Dan."

"Okay, Mom." Scarlett smiled. "Actually, I think they deserve one another."

Unamused, Zoe made a dismissive gesture.

"Hey, I was only kidding. Zoe? Have I touched a raw nerve?"

"What? No!" Zoe protested a bit too quickly.

"I guess opposites attract." Scarlett shrugged. "And I kind of like seeing Dan loosen up a little. Diego makes him seem almost tolerable."

Zoe shook her head and returned to her computer. "I'd better get back to work."

As she dove into some digital painting, Scarlett couldn't shake the feeling that Diego's arrival had shifted something in the office dynamic. She just wasn't sure what it was.

Scarlett reached for her phone, only to realize she'd left it in the conference room after the morning meeting. As she approached, she heard soft voices and slowed her steps, not wanting to interrupt if a meeting was still in progress.

"It's okay, honey. Just stay quiet and color while Mami finishes her work," a woman's voice said gently.

Scarlett peered around the corner and saw Maria, one of the night cleaning staff, kneeling beside a girl of about five or six. The child looked tired and on the verge of tears.

Maria looked over at someone Scarlett couldn't see. "I'm sorry. I know I'm not supposed to bring her, but my sister couldn't watch her tonight and—"

"Hey, it's all right," Dan's voice said, surprisingly gently. "These things happen. Is she hungry?"

Scarlett leaned a bit farther, catching sight of Dan crouched down to the little girl's eye level.

"Hi there," he said softly. "What's your name?"

"Lucia," the girl mumbled shyly.

"Nice to meet you, Lucia. I'm Dan. I don't know what I was thinking when I ordered this pizza, but it's way too much for me. Could you help me with this?"

Maria started to protest, but Dan held up a hand. "Please."

Scarlett leaned back against the wall and listened in amazement. This man was not the Dan Weston she knew—kind, patient, and unexpectedly good with children.

Remembering her phone, Scarlett stepped into the room to find Dan and Lucia happily chatting while eating pizza. He looked up, surprised, as Scarlett pointed at her phone. "Sorry. I, uh, forgot this."

He smiled and nodded then turned back to Lucia to resume their conversation.

As Scarlett left the room, something shifted inside her. Maybe there was more to Dan Weston than she'd initially thought.

She returned to her desk and lost herself in her work. Not until she heard Dan's frustrated sigh did she glance at her watch, at which point she was stunned to see that three hours had passed. Dan was staring at his screen, running his hands through his hair in a gesture of exasperation.

Before she could stop herself, Scarlett walked over to his desk. "Everything okay?" she asked, surprised by the concern in her own voice.

Dan looked up, startled, then composed himself. "Fine," he said, but Scarlett caught a flicker of something—pain?—in his eyes before his usual mask slipped back into place. "Just... reviewing some old data."

For a moment, Scarlett thought he might say more, but then he shook his head. "It's late. You should go home."

After hesitating for a moment, Scarlett asked, "Want a fresh pair of eyes?"

Dan's face lit up. "I didn't know you were a code jockey."

"I'm not, really. I just know enough to get myself into trouble—but not enough to get out of it. To be honest, I've got selfish motives. Seeing more of the app and your process might spark some ideas."

Dan shrugged and gestured toward a spare chair. Within minutes, Scarlett was surprised to notice how easily the two of them fell into a rhythm, discussing the code and Dan's vision for the look of the app. As they bounced ideas off each other, Scarlett found she could practically tolerate him. That was progress.

They were so immersed in their work that Diego's

return went unnoticed until he dramatically cleared his throat.

"Well, well, well. What do we have here? A little coding cumbia?" Diego launched into some hip-swiveling Latin dance moves.

Scarlett felt her cheeks heat up, suddenly aware of how closely she and Dan were sitting. She quickly stood up and smoothed down her shirt. "We were just working on a bug."

Diego waggled his eyebrows suggestively. "Is that what the kids are calling it these days?"

Dan shot his friend a warning look. "Diego..."

"All right, all right." Diego held up his hands in surrender. "Far be it from me to interrupt the sacred act of debugging. But Dan, my man, you promised me a night out. Don't tell me you're bailing on me for some lines of code?"

Dan looked torn, glancing between his computer and his expectant friend.

Scarlett surprised herself by saying, "Go ahead, Dan. We can pick this up tomorrow." As soon as the words were out, she regretted them. Dan didn't need her permission, and she fully expected to hear as much at any moment.

"I hate leaving a problem unsolved," Dan said.

She nodded and managed a small smile. "Yeah, I know. But it'll still be here in the morning."

"Unlike your youth!" Diego interjected. "Come on, Dan. The night is young, and so are we... ish."

Dan chuckled, shaking his head as he stood up. "All right, all right. Let me just grab my jacket."

As Dan gathered his belongings, Diego turned to Scarlett. "You're joining us, aren't you?"

The question took her aback. "Oh, um, thanks, but I've got some loose ends to tie up."

Diego shrugged. "Suit yourself."

Dan pulled his keys from his pocket. "Ready to go?"

As they headed toward the exit, Dan paused and looked back at Scarlett. "Thanks for your help today. I'll see you tomorrow."

Scarlett nodded, feeling a strange swirl of emotions she couldn't quite understand. "Yeah. See you tomorrow."

She watched as the two men left, Diego with his arm slung around Dan's shoulders, already regaling him with some outrageous story.

The office felt oddly quiet in their wake.

4

When the hum of the office had wound down, a determined Zoe all but dragged Scarlett out of the office.

"Come on," Zoe insisted with a hint of desperation. "After that lunch, I need a drink. And you, my friend, need to spill about what's going on with you and Dan."

Scarlett sputtered, "Going on? We work together."

Zoe rolled her eyes as she and Scarlett stepped into the elevator. "Sure. Uh-huh. And those sparks? Must be a hot CPU!"

Before Scarlett could protest further, a hurried coworker stuck a hand in front of the elevator door and joined them for a silent ride to the ground floor.

Minutes later, Scarlett and Zoe arrived at the 404 Tavern, a trendy spot popular with the tech crowd. The two of them found a quiet booth in the corner and ordered their drinks—a light beer for Scarlett and an electric blue cocktail for Zoe.

Once the friends were settled, Zoe leaned forward,

her eyes sparkling with curiosity. "Okay, spill. What's the deal with you and Mr. Tall, Dark, and Geeksome?"

Scarlett sighed, tracing the rim of her glass, unsure how to describe the conflicting emotions Dan stirred in her. "Okay. Honestly? I don't know. One moment, I hate him and his project, then the next moment, his ridiculous enthusiasm wins me over." She winced. "And... sometimes I find myself looking and longing..."

Zoe shrugged. "At that face? Who wouldn't?"

"And that butt."

Sagely, Zoe nodded. "Ah, the classic 'I hate you—I want you' dilemma."

"It's not... like you're making it sound," Scarlett protested weakly. "It's just... complicated."

For a moment, Zoe frowned. "Is it? 'Cause—and this is just my theory—people say that, but the truth is, it usually isn't."

Scarlett shook her head. "Then why do I feel so confused?"

Zoe looked almost sad. "Because that's how you feel when..."

Scarlett waited as long as she could. "When what?"

Zoe's eyes softened. "When you're falling in love."

Scarlett stared blankly. "Well, that's... crazy! Besides, this is work. We spend time together because we have to. It's called being professional. That's all."

Across the room, laughter erupted from where Diego was telling one of his stories. Zoe grew unnaturally quiet, her eyes fixed on him. A blend of emotions played across her face—longing, hurt, anger.

"Zo?" Scarlett whispered. "You okay?"

Zoe blinked as if coming out of a trance. "Yeah, I'm fine." But her smile didn't reach her eyes. "It's just... having him around brings back memories, you know?"

"Good ones or bad ones?"

"Both." The laugh Zoe emitted was tinged with sadness. "That's what makes it so hard." She sighed. "Diego... approaches life the same way he attacks code —with absolute confidence and just enough chaos to keep things interesting." With a knowing look, she explained, "Typical rock climber—always seeking the next challenge, the next rush, the next impossible feat to conquer—like me."

Scarlett felt a pang of sympathy as she realized this matter was about more than just work.

Zoe glanced down, frowning, but she continued. "As random as he seems, he has an uncanny ability to see patterns others miss, both in code and in people, which is part of the problem. That same restless energy that makes him brilliant at solving problems also makes him terrible at facing them—especially when they come in the form of honest emotions."

Scarlett tried not to wince. As Diego's gaze met Zoe's across the room, the air seemed to crackle with unresolved tension. Scarlett suddenly felt like she was intruding on a private moment, one loaded with a history she didn't yet understand. But Diego averted his eyes, and the moment ended. He was laughing again with his pals.

Zoe smiled but not in a good way. "I'm not saying work is the worst place to fall for a guy, but take a good look at me. This could be you in a year. And then, no matter what happens, he'll be there every day—breaking your heart until he asks for a transfer and leaves you in your cubicle with your broken heart bleeding all over your computer peripherals. And then, just when you think you're over him, he comes back."

"Oh, Zoe, I'm sorry!"

With a slight shake of her head, Zoe said, "A year. It's been a whole year. What sort of person can't get over a guy in a year?"

Scarlett gazed sympathetically. "Which is why this whole Dan thing is a nonstarter. I've got enough angst with work. After the Tax Tykes disaster, I can't afford another failure. I've got to focus on work, not on... whatever this is with Dan."

Zoe's expression softened. "Hey, Tax Tykes wasn't your fault. Who could have predicted that kids wouldn't find accounting exciting?" A smile teased her lips.

Scarlett groaned and buried her face in her hands. "If you'll recall, the app was not my brainchild. But a good graphic designer should have been able to come up with a vision that worked."

Zoe wrinkled her nose. "Really? I don't know... I think you need special glasses for that kind of vision."

Scarlett stared dejectedly into the distance.

Zoe nudged Scarlett with her elbow. "Come on. There are so many people ahead of you in the blame line. Frankly, I blame marketing for deciding to sell it as the next *Assassin's Creed*."

"Yeah, at least I talked them out of calling it Accountant's Creed."

"Good call." Now squinting, Zoe tilted her head. "Tax Tykes was so much better."

Scarlett turned back to Zoe. "But was it?"

Zoe opened her mouth, but no answer came out. The pair burst into laughter.

"Thanks, Zo."

Zoe winced.

"No, really. Big points for effort! And I needed a laugh." But as the words emerged, she grew serious. "There's too much riding on this project."

Zoe took a long sip of her electric blue concoction. "I know. On the bright side, maybe Dan's—"

"Shh!"

"Why?"

"Don't look now."

Zoe's head swiveled around toward the door, where Dan spied her, smiled, and waved at her.

Scarlett glared at her friend. "What does 'don't look' mean to you?"

Donning her most apologetic expression, Zoe said, "Sorry. I just—sorry."

Diego soon joined him and, alerted by Dan, looked over at Scarlett and Zoe and also waved.

With a plastered-on smile, Zoe said, "Great. Here they come. This is my lucky day." She took a healthy swig of her drink.

Scarlett sighed. "Well, it's kind of the only bar close to work, so the odds were pretty good we'd run into them here."

Zoe's face lit up—except for her eyes. "Hey guys!"

Diego smiled. Scarlett had to admit, the guy had a

great smile and dark eyes a girl could get lost in—not this girl, not Zoe's friend, but any other woman with a pulse could. It didn't matter because the guy was laser-focused on Zoe, which didn't appear to escape Dan's notice.

Dan gripped his buddy's shoulder. "How 'bout that pool game?"

From the way Dan tightened his grip on a reluctant Diego's shoulder, Scarlett sensed Dan knew far more of the story than she did.

Zoe took a drink, shuddered as if to shake off the encounter, then watched the guys walk away. The women silently watched the pool game for a bit until Zoe broke the silence. "You're right about one thing. That Dan of yours—"

"Shh! He's not mine, and be quiet. He'll hear you!"

Zoe laughed and made a sweeping gesture toward the crowded bar. "In here?"

"Okay, fine. Maybe I'm a tiny bit paranoid."

Zoe's eyes twinkled. "Just a bit. But you bring up a good point. What we need is a nickname so we can talk about him undetected."

Scarlett shook her head. "Or maybe not talk about him at all."

Undeterred, Zoe narrowed her eyes for a moment as she pivoted around and watched Dan lean over the pool table, his cue poised for a shot. Her eyes brightened. "I know! Butt Boy!"

Scarlett grimaced. "I am not going to call him Butt Boy!"

"But you said he had a nice—"

After administering a sharp kick to Zoe's foot, Scarlett looked up and smiled. "Dan! Hi!"

Zoe muttered, "That was quick."

"What?" The confused look on Dan's face relaxed as Diego approached. Once everyone else told him what they were all drinking, he headed for the bar to get another round.

Dan turned to Zoe. "So..." Before he could continue, his phone rang. With a helpless shrug, he headed for the door, covering one ear.

Zoe studied the view. "The moniker fits him. And so do those pants."

"Zoe!" Catching a glimpse as he walked out the door, however, Scarlett had to admit her friend wasn't wrong. Still, she needed to change the subject before it devolved further. "So, what's the story with you and Diego?" When Zoe hesitated, Scarlett added, "There's obviously more history there than you've told me."

Zoe's usual bubbly demeanor deflated. "Oh, that. That's... a long and complicated story."

"Somebody once told me—ten minutes ago—that nothing's that complicated," Scarlett said gently.

"I never said 'nothing.'" Zoe took a deep breath and heaved a huge sigh. "Okay, fine. Here goes. Diego and I... were engaged."

Scarlett's eyes widened. "What? When?"

"A year ago," Zoe said, her voice soft with remembrance.

"But you never said anything!"

A pained look on her face, Zoe nodded. "I know. We met at work, obviously. He walked in one day—this brilliant, wild coder who could make computers—and my heart—dance. I was... well, me. I fell hard and fast."

Scarlett paused for a moment. "I knew you guys got along really well."

Zoe rolled her eyes. "Really well. But he didn't want anyone at work to know. Office gossip and whatnot."

"So, what happened?" Scarlett asked, trying not to look too eager. But engaged? She would never have guessed that.

Again, Zoe's laugh was tinged with sadness. "Life happened. Or, more accurately, reality did. The engagement—if that's what it ever really was—came out of a casual 'what if' kind of conversation. We'd both had a few, and one minute we were talking about the future. It was all hypothetical. I said I could see myself maybe getting a master's and maybe working my way up to director. Then, out of the blue, he said, 'I could see myself married to you.'"

"What?!"

"That's what I said! And with pretty much the same shocked expression."

Scarlett shook her head slowly. "I would never have thought—"

Zoe's eyes shimmered. "I waited for him to say he was kidding, but he didn't. It was almost like someone else said it, and then he agreed. 'Yeah, I could see us together.' Of course, knowing Diego, I didn't dare believe him. He could've just backed out right then, but it was like this big curtain opened—a heavy velvet theater curtain—and revealed the real guy, the Diego that no one else saw." She looked down and said softly, "Except me." With a quick swipe of her wrist, she brushed away tears. But more followed.

Grabbing a cocktail napkin and dabbing her eyes, Zoe took a deep breath and let it out as if she could exhale her emotions. "The thing about Diego that's so exhilarating and terrifying is his complete lack of fear. He'll try anything. Without hesitation, he'll just jump in and do it, which in this case meant marrying me."

"Oh, Zoe." Scarlett squeezed her friend's shoulder.

"But that's not the worst part. Like an idiot, I said yes!"

"That's so..."

"Pitiful? Oh, believe me, I know."

Scarlett still couldn't believe what she was hearing. "I was going to say unexpected—and romantic."

Zoe looked at her blankly. "In a pitiful way."

"No. I just... I had no idea."

"No one did—not even Dan."

Recalling how, earlier, Dan whisked Diego away, Scarlett said, "Are you sure?"

"Oh, Dan knows we had a thing, but there's no way Diego would have mentioned the engagement."

"How could you not share the news?"

A bitter light flickered in Zoe's eyes. "We stayed up for a while and imagined how it would be. We even talked about children." Her face wrinkled in pain, but she took another deep breath and continued. "Then we woke up the next morning. He didn't mention it once. We had coffee and walked to the diner. It was a beautiful, bright Sunday morning. The only others outside were a couple of joggers, a woman walking a dog, and so many couples in love. We were supposed to be one of those couples, but I knew that we weren't."

Scarlett couldn't imagine the situation. "But you must've talked more about it."

Zoe rolled her eyes and nodded. "I wish that we hadn't. I waited until after breakfast, and we were safely back home." She laughed bitterly. "Home. My home, not his. Then I asked him."

Scarlett shook her head, heart aching for Zoe.

"By then, I'd convinced myself that he didn't remember, but he did. 'Zo, we got over our skis.'

"'I'm a pretty good skier,' I said.

"He looked into my eyes with those dark eyes I got lost in and said, 'But I'm not.'

"That was pretty much it. He gave me a hug—like a consolation prize for a game-show contestant. But I took it. I buried myself in his chest and breathed in... Diego. I took in his scent and clung close to his unreachable heart. Then, a quick kiss on the forehead later, he was gone. Out the door. Out of my life. Except that proposal did something to me. It opened my heart and let love rush in like a tide. And go out, leaving a vast wasteland of soggy sand for the clams and me to burrow into."

Scarlett tried not to smile. "And you still had to work with him."

"Oh yeah. Because once wasn't enough. He had to go on breaking my heart, day after day."

"So that's why he transferred?"

"Oh, no—not to spare me! Him, maybe. I think seeing me was a reminder of his narrow escape. Like the stories he tells, I was just another adventure, a close brush with the horror of marrying me."

Now Scarlett felt angry. "What a crappy guy-thing to do."

"I'm sure he never wanted to hurt me. I was just another adrenaline rush until he caught me, and the adventure was over. I'm just another fish he threw back into the sea."

Scarlett would have laughed if Zoe hadn't looked so pitifully mournful. She raised a hand to get the bartender's attention then pointed at Zoe's glass with a nod.

Zoe sighed. "So, two months later, he vanished—just didn't show up to work. I figured he was home sick or, more likely, hungover. But when he didn't show up the next day, I asked Dan. The look in his eyes made it worse. He'd known for weeks, but Diego swore him to secrecy. He got a transfer—a lateral one—no raise, no promotion. The only perk was the distance from me."

Scarlett reached across the table and squeezed Zoe's hand. "Oh, Zo. I'm so sorry."

Zoe managed a weak smile. "It's okay. I mean, it wasn't for a long time. But I've moved on. Built a life for myself. Except now..."

"Now he's back," Scarlett finished.

"Yeah," Zoe sighed. "And... I don't know. All the things I imagined I'd feel aren't even close to how I feel now. Part of me wants to throw my drink at him, and the other part wants to throw myself at him."

"Oh," Scarlett replied gently.

"Yeah." Zoe nodded, her face full of self-loathing. "I'm actually a very smart person—except for my heart."

Scarlett shook her head. "It's not stupid. It's human."

They sat in companionable silence for a moment, each lost in her own thoughts.

Finally, Zoe straightened up, a determined look on her face. "Okay, enough wallowing. Here's to life without men!"

Scarlett raised her glass in a toast. "Hear, hear!"

As they clinked glasses, Scarlett couldn't help but feel a twinge of doubt. She glanced over at Dan, who was laughing at something Diego had said.

Life without men? I like men. Dammit, I like... Dan. So what? It's just a crush... just a harmless crush.

5

The next morning, Scarlett paused at her desk chair and looked down the aisle between cubicles. Dan's desk was empty. That was different. She checked her watch and confirmed that it was well past the time he usually arrived. Deciding he must be in an early meeting, she settled into her own workspace, determined to make progress on ChronicleMe.

She was on her way back to her desk with her first cup of coffee when a disheveled Dan stumbled in, followed closely by an equally rumpled Diego.

"Morning, sunshine," Diego called out cheerfully, seemingly unaffected by what appeared to have been a late night.

Dan groaned, slumping into his chair. "Inside voice, Diego. Please."

Scarlett couldn't help but smirk. "Rough night?"

Dan looked up, his eyes bleary. "Yeah. My friend here decided we needed to 'paint the town red,' but it was more of a tequila-tinged gold."

Diego flashed an unrepentant grin. "Life's too short for moderation. Besides, you can't tell me you didn't have fun."

Before Dan could respond, Zoe breezed down the hallway, her arms full of colorful folders. She stopped short when she saw Diego, and her usual cheerful expression faltered for a split second.

"Diego," she said, her voice a mixture of surprise and something else Scarlett couldn't quite identify.

Diego smiled again, but now it looked forced. "Zoe."

An awkward silence fell over the group. Scarlett wished she could melt into her chair and vanish.

Dan cleared his throat and turned to Diego. "I've got work to do."

"Oh, right. Lunch." Diego turned toward Zoe and Scarlett. "Join us. The more the merrier."

Scarlett seriously doubted that, but she couldn't think of a way to say no, inadvertently leaving the task to Zoe.

"I don't think so," Zoe said softly and turned toward her cube.

Diego spread his arms wide. "Come on, Zo. For old times' sake? I promise to be on my best behavior."

Zoe snorted. "Your best behavior's not always enough."

Diego clutched his heart dramatically. "Ouch."

Stunned, Scarlett watched the exchange, feeling helpless to rescue her friend.

"Fine," Zoe said, her tone missing its usual zest. "But only if Scarlett comes too."

All eyes turned to Scarlett, who felt like a deer caught in headlights.

"I..." With an awkward point at her desk, she said, "There's this... thing I was going to do." When her eyes met Zoe's, which pleaded silently but intensely, Scarlett did a quick pivot. "But I could really use a break."

"Excellent!" Diego clapped his hands together. "We'll be by to pick you up later."

As the guys headed for their desks, Scarlett sank into her chair beside Zoe. "You okay?" she whispered.

Zoe nodded, but her usual bounce was noticeably absent. "Yeah, just... thanks for coming. I owe you one."

Three hours later, they wound up at a nearby taco joint and crammed into a small booth. After Zoe urged Scarlett into the booth, Zoe practically body-checked Dan and slid in beside her. Dan took a seat across from Scarlett, leaving Diego across from Zoe, where he regaled them with stories of his latest adventures.

"So, there I was, hanging off the side of this cliff in Yosemite," Diego was saying, gesticulating wildly, "when I realized I'd left my good-luck charm back at the campsite. Now, most people would just shrug and keep climbing, but not me. I—"

"Let me guess," Zoe interrupted, her voice dripping with sarcasm. "You decided to free-solo back down, sprint to the campsite, grab your lucky rabbit's foot or whatever, and then climb back up. All before breakfast."

Diego grinned. "Close! Not a rabbit's foot, but my lucky..." He paused. For a moment, his bravura cleared like a mist, leaving him looking uncharacteristically vulnerable. "My, uh, Linux penguin keyring stress ball."

Zoe looked up and stared straight at Diego, who looked everywhere but at her.

Dan shook his head, a mix of admiration and exasperation on his face. "You're insane, you know that?"

"Insanely badass?" Diego corrected.

Scarlett couldn't help but notice the way Zoe's knuckles whitened as she gripped her glass. There was definitely more to that story.

Attempting to change the subject, Scarlett turned to Dan. "So, how's the pattern-recognition module coming along? Any breakthroughs?"

Dan's face lit up, and Scarlett felt a slight flutter in her chest at his enthusiasm. "Actually, yes! I woke up, and I swear it just came to me! A recursive neural network! I implemented it this morning, and poof! Problem solved!"

"Whoa, whoa, whoa," Diego interrupted. "No shop talk at the lunch table. That's a cardinal rule, my friends."

Dan rolled his eyes. "Since when do you care about rules?"

"Since they align with my interests," Diego replied with a wink. "Now, who wants to hear about the time I accidentally joined a traveling circus in Budapest?"

As Diego launched into another improbable tale, Scarlett caught Zoe's eye. Her friend looked uncomfortable, almost pained. Without thinking, Scarlett reached under the table and gave Zoe's hand a quick squeeze. Zoe shot her a grateful look.

The rest of lunch passed in a blur of Diego's stories, Dan's occasional attempts to steer the conversation back to work, and Zoe's uncharacteristic silence. By the time the group headed back to the office, Scarlett's head was spinning with questions.

As they entered the building, Diego suddenly announced, "Well, this has been fun, but I've got places to be."

Dan eyed Diego skeptically. "Places?"

"HR. Hey, with any luck, we'll all be cube buddies!"

Zoe muttered, "That would be some luck."

Clapping a hand on Dan's shoulder, Diego said, "Dan, don't work too hard. Scarlett, keep him in line for me." He turned to Zoe, his expression softening. "Zo, it was good to see you."

With an unreadable expression, Zoe met his gaze. "Take care of yourself."

After a final wave, Diego sauntered off, leaving a wake of confusion behind him.

Awkward silence settled over the group as they rode the elevator back to their floor. Dan cleared his throat. "So, that was... interesting."

Zoe let out a short, humorless laugh. "That's one word for it."

The elevator dinged, signaling their arrival. As they stepped out, Dan turned to Zoe. "Hey, I'm sorry about Diego. If I'd known..."

Zoe managed a small smile. "It's not your fault. Diego is... Diego. Unfortunately."

As they returned to their desks, Scarlett glanced

over at Zoe, who was uncharacteristically somber as she booted up her computer.

Scarlett hesitated then asked the question that had been burning in her mind. "So, Zoe, you and Diego..."

Zoe sighed, her shoulders slumping. "Yeah. Me and Diego." She shuddered. "But enough about me. What's going on with you two?"

Scarlett tried to look confused, but the knowing look in Zoe's eyes stopped her short.

"Well okay. It's weird," she mused. "At first, I thought Dan was just another arrogant tech bro. But now..."

"Now?" Zoe prompted, the knowing glint still in her eye.

Scarlett sighed. "Now I'm not so sure. There are moments when he lets his guard down, and I see this... *passion*... dedication. He's got something you so seldom see anymore."

A mischievous twinkle lit Zoe's eyes. "In his *pants*?"

Scarlett leveled a look. "Integrity."

"Wow. That is *not* where I thought you were going with that!"

"Should I ask?"

"Do you really need to? 'Cause I think you know. Someone's got a crush," Zoe teased.

"It's not a crush," Scarlett protested, but even as she said it, she wasn't sure she believed it. "It's just... you know."

"No. Not really." Zoe looked almost serious.

With a shrug, Scarlett said, "No. Neither do I."

A FEW DAYS after the awkward lunch with Diego, Scarlett was buried in work when Dan cleared his throat, startling her.

"Hey, Scarlett," he said, his voice uncharacteristically hesitant. "Do you have a minute?"

She looked up, surprised by his tone. "Sure, what's up?"

Dan glanced around the office then lowered his voice. "I was hoping we could talk privately. About the project. Would you mind meeting me at the cafe downstairs in about fifteen minutes?"

Scarlett's brow furrowed. "Oh... okay. Is everything all right?"

"Yeah, yeah," Dan assured her quickly. "I just want to discuss something without the whole team around."

As Dan walked away, Scarlett knew something was off. She tried to focus on her work for the next few minutes, but her mind kept wandering to what Dan might want to discuss.

Fifteen minutes later, Scarlett found herself pushing open the door to the cafe. She spotted Dan immediately. He was hunched over his laptop at a corner table. As she approached, she noticed the tense set of his shoulders.

"Hey," she said, sliding into the seat across from him. "So, what's up?"

Dan looked up, his expression melding discomfort with determination. "I wanted to run a test of the

ChronicleMe app," he began, "but I ran into a bit of... well, a challenge."

Scarlett raised an eyebrow. "A challenge?"

Dan nodded, turning his laptop so she could see the screen. "I tried to use your social media accounts as a test case, but I could hardly find anything. At first, I thought there might be a bug in the algorithm, but then I realized..."

"That I'm not exactly an open book online," Scarlett finished for him, a wry smile on her face.

"Exactly," Dan said, looking relieved that she wasn't offended. "I figured it might be better to discuss this privately rather than with the whole team."

Scarlett felt an unexpected wave of gratitude toward Dan. It was surprisingly considerate of him to approach this subject delicately. "I appreciate that," she said softly.

Dan's expression softened. "I know not everyone is comfortable putting their whole life online. But I did manage to gather some data, and I wanted to show you the results before sharing them with anyone else."

He turned the laptop back toward himself and clicked a few times before spinning it around to face Scarlett again. "Take a look."

Scarlett leaned forward, and her eyes scanned the screen. At first, she saw what she expected—a sparse collection of data points from her limited social media presence. But as she continued reading, her heart began to race.

There, on the screen, were references to events she had never shared online. A broken long-term relationship that had left her heart in pieces. A series of impressive art scholarships and awards she'd received in college. The beginnings of what looked like a promising career trajectory in the art world.

And then... nothing.

Scarlett sat back, her mind reeling. "How... how did the app find all this?"

Dan looked both impressed and a little sheepish. "The algorithm doesn't just look at your posts. It analyzes mentions of you in other people's posts, tags in photos, even public records. It's designed to build a comprehensive picture, even with limited direct input."

Scarlett nodded numbly, still staring at the screen. She saw her life laid out before her, including the parts she'd tried to keep hidden.

Dan's voice was gentle when he spoke again. "I'm sorry. I don't mean to pry. I honestly just meant to take the app for a test run. But it is quite a story—an impressive one!"

Scarlett sighed, running a hand through her hair. "No, not really. I was strikingly mediocre at pretty much everything I ever attempted except art. It's not like I ever had a moment where I decided that's what I was going to do with my life. I just did it because I loved it. And for a while, it looked like it was meant to be. I got a few scholarships and awards."

"A few?" Dan gestured wide-eyed at the screen. "I mean, look at this list of accomplishments!"

She paused, swallowing hard against the lump forming in her throat. "Yeah... but it just... it never panned out. The art world is competitive and... Maybe talent isn't always enough. You need contacts, exposure, a good business sense... luck? Whatever it takes, the planets never aligned. So I shifted my focus to rent and the occasional meal."

Dan became quiet, his eyes studying her face. "That must have been difficult," he said finally. "But you're still making art. Everyone here loves your work."

Scarlett thought she'd fall out of her chair. *Who are you? 'Cause you're not the Dan Weston we all know and work with.* She recovered and shrugged off the shock, despite the emotion welling up inside her. "Well, thanks. I, uh—thanks."

His voice softened. "So, let's round off the rough edges and make it into something we can share with the group. Meanwhile, I'll work on incorporating more editing options for end users. It's actually a good thing that this happened."

It doesn't feel good to me.

He continued. "It's opened my eyes to some potential hiccups in the user experience, which we'll want to avoid."

Great. My life is reduced to a hiccup.

"Yeah..." Dan said, as if thinking out loud. "We need more robust privacy controls and a way for people to choose the depth of research and final product. Hmm..."

They sat in silence for a moment, the hum of the surrounding cafe providing a gentle backdrop to their thoughts.

Finally, Dan spoke again. "Anyway, I hope you don't mind me saying this, but I think you're amazing."

He quickly added, "Your work... I mean, I'm glad you're on the team." Their eyes met, and something shifted between them. It felt as though a cloud had passed over Dan and, for the first time, revealed a clear look at him. The feeling was oddly powerful—unsettling—as a warmth spread through her chest. She averted her eyes and barely whispered, "Thanks."

Suddenly, the old businesslike Dan closed his laptop. "Well. Back to work."

As they gathered their possessions to return to the office, Scarlett wondered what had just happened. Was this the real Dan Weston? Beneath that brusque, robotic persona, was he hiding a thoughtful, empathetic human?

6

The following day found Dan and Diego perched on metal stools at a rickety table at a bustling food truck park. Dan picked at his fish tacos while Diego scarfed down a towering burger.

"So," Dan began, wiping his hands on a napkin, "you want to tell me what that was all about yesterday? With Zoe?"

Diego slowed his chewing and swallowed hard. "Ah, that. It's... you know. History."

Dan leveled a weary look. "Yeah, I know your history. But this is Zoe, my friend."

Sighing, Diego put down his burger. "Fair enough. Zoe and I... had a thing."

Dan raised an eyebrow. "A thing."

"Yeah, well..." Diego averted his eyes. "We were engaged."

Dan nearly choked on his taco. "Engaged? You said a thing. A thing is—it's like a one-nighter."

"Well, it was a one-nighter, and another, and another... you know."

"No, not really." Dan eyed Diego skeptically.

"We were together. Briefly."

"Vertically or horizontally?"

Diego glared. "For a couple of months."

"A couple of months?"

Diego shifted his position. "Yeah." When Dan was silent, Diego added, "It happens."

"It happens?"

"Yeah! Do you have to repeat everything I say?"

Dan shrugged. "Only the parts where you're lying."

"Hey!" He sounded clearly defensive. "I'm not lying!"

"Not to anyone else, except maybe Zoe. But to yourself? Absolutely."

Diego slumped his shoulders in defeat. "Okay, fine. I liked her." He caught Dan's look, widened his eyes as though he might explode, and then threw his hands into the air. "I loved her, okay?"

Dan didn't feel as victorious as he should have. "I've known you for years, and I've never seen you commit, let alone admit you have feelings."

"I've got feelings!" Diego fired back. His usual jovial expression faltered. "But, well... Zoe was different. She was... she is... incredible. Smart, funny, beautiful. And she can spot that elusive piece of missing code that makes everything run perfectly, you know?"

Dan nodded. "She sure had you figured out."

Diego's eyes clouded over. "Yeah."

"So, she's incredible, smart, funny, and beautiful. No wonder it didn't work out."

Diego drew a deep breath and then exhaled. "She got me. I didn't have to pretend. She saw through all that—"

"Crap?" Dan raised an eyebrow.

Diego didn't try to argue. "Whatever."

"So, she got you. You loved her. And for reasons I'll never understand, she managed to tolerate you. Sounds pretty perfect to me."

"Yeah, it was."

"So, you and this bright, hilarious, and cute little hottie were in love and engaged to be married."

"For about ten minutes, total."

Dan nodded. "And you...?" The truth dawned on Dan, and his face reflected the realization. "You got scared and ran, didn't you?"

Diego shut his eyes for a moment. "It got suddenly real—and too close."

"So you broke her heart." Dan stared blankly at his plate.

"I know, I know." Diego held up his hands. "I messed up. Biggest mistake of my life. I've regretted it every day since."

Dan raised his eyes and stared at the horizon. "It's a good thing you didn't tell me this back then." He glanced at Diego's questioning look. "Because I'd have decked you."

Their eyes met. To Diego's credit, he didn't crack a hint of a smile. They both knew Dan was no match for Diego, but Diego also had to know that wouldn't have stopped Dan from trying. Dan shook his head in disgust.

Diego ran a hand through his hair. "If it makes you feel any better, I've spent the last year beating myself up more than you ever could."

Dan fell quiet and took a moment to process this new information. "Is that why you're really here? To win her back?"

Diego shrugged, a mix of hope and resignation on his face. "No, the transfer was corporate's decision. But seeing her again... It brought everything back. I guess this is my punishment. I know she'll never forgive me."

Dan leaned back, studying his friend. "So here you are."

"Yup. Who knows? Maybe she'll finally see what a jerk I really am."

Dan smirked. "She could ask me. I've known that for years." They both laughed, and the tension between them dissipated.

Diego mused. "What about you?"

"Me? I'm not a jerk."

Diego leveled a look. "That's one opinion." Amusement lit his eyes. "But seriously, I saw the way you were looking at Scarlett."

It was Dan's turn to look uncomfortable. "Who, Scarlett, my professional colleague? We're not... I can't..."

"Can't what?" Diego leaned closer, flashed a smarmy smile, and confided, "You know they make pills for that, right?"

"Very funny." Dan sighed, his shoulders slumping.

"I can't let myself go there, Diego. ChronicleMe... it's not just another app for me. It's everything."

"What do you mean? Like a Swiss Army knife scrapbook combo?"

Dan gave a brief glance to Diego before leaning back and staring off into the distance. "You remember Mandy, my sister?"

Diego nodded, barely able to contain his amusement. "Yeah, sure! Mandy, the good-looking, smart one, as opposed to her poor brother Dan."

"She was smart. And funny."

"Wait. Was?" Diego was suddenly somber, a rare moment for him.

With a grim nod, Dan said, "She was pulling an all-nighter to study for finals, so she took an Adderall. She didn't know it was laced with fentanyl."

Diego's eyes widened in shock. "No... Dan, I didn't know. I'm so sorry."

Dan nodded again, blinking back tears. "She was so full of life. Unlike her older brother, she was good at everything she attempted. The line at the funeral wrapped around the block. People we never knew came to share little stories—how she'd touched their lives in small and big ways. Things we never knew."

A look of dawning understanding bloomed on Diego's face. "And that's where ChronicleMe came from."

Dan nodded. "I wanted to create something that could help people understand themselves better and be shared with their loved ones."

"That's... wow, Dan. That's incredible," Diego said softly.

"But it also means I can't afford any distractions," Dan continued. "This has to work. I owe it to Mandy. And if it fails..." He trailed off, unable to finish the thought.

"It won't." Diego leveled a confident look at him. "And file this under 'Do what I say, not what I do,' but maybe letting someone in, someone like Scarlett, could actually help."

That assertion drew a hesitant smile from Dan.

Diego grinned. "And, of course, you've got me!"

"Lucky me."

"The main thing is, you don't have to do this alone."

Dan managed a weak smile. "Yeah. Food for thought."

"Speaking of food..." Diego dug back into his tacos.

Both men sat in contemplative silence, wrestling with their own fears and regrets.

DIEGO'S ADVICE seemed stuck in a loop that replayed in his mind through the hours that followed. *Maybe letting someone in, someone like Scarlett, could actually help.* Dan shook his head, trying to focus on the code in front of him, but Diego's words kept intruding.

The office had long since emptied, nothing breaking the silence but the quiet hum of electronics. Dan rubbed his eyes, realizing he'd lost track of time again.

He glanced at the clock—past midnight. Although he knew he should go home, the thought of his empty apartment held little appeal.

A movement caught his eye, and he looked up to see Scarlett standing by his cubicle partition. Her red hair was slightly mussed, and her cheek had a smudge of what looked like graphite. Probably from her sketching, he thought, surprised at how endearing he found it.

"Hey, workaholic. You do know it's past midnight, right?" Her voice was soft, teasing.

Despite his exhaustion, Dan felt a smile tugging at his lips. "I could say the same to you. What are you still doing here?"

Scarlett shrugged, stepping into his office. "Lost track of time. But I think I've finally cracked the UI for the new privacy features."

She held out her tablet, and Dan stood. He moved around his desk to get a better look. As he leaned in, he suddenly realized how close they were standing. He caught a whiff of shampoo—something floral and fresh.

"This is brilliant, Scarlett," he murmured, genuinely impressed by her work. He looked up and found himself face-to-face with her. "You're brilliant."

For a moment, they just stood there as the air between them seemed charged with unspoken possibilities. Dan's gaze dropped to Scarlett's lips, and he suddenly wondered what it would be like to kiss her. Diego's words echoed in his mind again: "You don't have to do this alone."

With an effort, Dan stepped back, running a hand

through his hair. "We, uh, we should probably call it a night."

Scarlett nodded, but—was it his imagination, or did she look a little disappointed? "Right. Early meeting tomorrow."

As they gathered their belongings and headed for the elevator, a strange mix of regret and relief washed over Dan. He wanted to reach out to Scarlett to let her in, as Diego had suggested. But the memory of Mandy and the pain of losing someone he loved held him back.

In the elevator, the silence between the two of them felt charged with unspoken words. When they reached the lobby, Dan turned to Scarlett, feeling an inexplicable need to say something more. "Scarlett, I..."

She looked up at him, her green eyes curious and maybe a little hopeful. "Yes?"

For a moment, a scene flashed through his mind. In his imagination, he threw caution to the wind and blurted out how he felt, how much Scarlett's presence on the team meant to him. How much she meant to him.

But fear won out. Instead, Dan shook his head and managed a rueful smile. "Never mind. Goodnight, Scarlett."

"Goodnight, Dan," she replied softly and walked away into the night.

As Dan proceeded to his car, he knew he'd missed out on something important, and he felt its loss. But, he convinced himself, ChronicleMe had to come first. He couldn't afford any distractions, no matter how tempting they might be. Still, as he drove home, his mind kept drifting back to Scarlett's smile, and he found himself looking forward to seeing her again in the morning.

7

S carlett arrived at the office early, eager to try some new concepts that had come to her while driving to work. As she settled into her desk, she noticed Dan's workspace was still empty. Scarlett's thoughts strayed from the task at hand, but she pushed them aside and booted up her computer.

Zoe appeared, looking uncharacteristically somber once more. "Hey," she said, perching on the edge of Scarlett's desk. "Uh... when you and Dan ran a ChronicleMe report on yourselves, did anything... unexpected come up?"

Scarlett opened her mouth but couldn't find the right words.

Zoe, apparently taking that as a no, continued. "Because..." She bit her lip. "I tried it last night, and it was... intense. It dug up some stuff I thought I'd buried."

Scarlett leaned closer. "About Diego?"

Zoe grimaced. "And other things... people. It's scary

how much it pieced together. I mean, don't get me wrong. I love social media. But I always thought I controlled it—more or less." She shook her head.

Dan walked by, looking tired but determined. Nodding toward both women, he sat at his desk.

Scarlett turned back to Zoe. "So, are you okay?"

"Yeah. Maybe. It was just... a lot." Zoe managed a small smile. "Anyway, I think we might need to have a conversation about it at our next meeting. I mean, not all memories should be scrapbooked on acid-free paper."

As Zoe walked away, Scarlett stared at the ChronicleMe icon on her desktop. She'd been putting off digging into her story, but with the meeting approaching, it had to be done. With a deep breath, she clicked the app open.

The interface was clean and inviting, just like she'd designed it. So far, so good. She opened her file and waited as the app processed her data. Before long, a timeline appeared on her screen, peppered with photos, posts, and events from her past.

Scarlett scrolled through, surprised at how much the app had gleaned from her sparse online presence. She paused at a photo from her college graduation. The app had somehow linked it to her class rank and displayed her achievements alongside the image.

As she delved deeper, the familiar pattern she knew all too well became clear. It had picked up on her tendency to withdraw from social media during a specific time of the year, correlating it with the anniversary of her father's passing. Scarlett felt a lump form in her throat. She'd never thought her grief could be so visible. Confronted with the fact of it now, she realized that was when her gradual withdrawal from social media began.

A notification popped up. "New connection discovered." Intrigued, Scarlett clicked on it.

Her eyes widened as she saw a series of interactions between her and Dan, dating back to when she first joined the company. Casual exchanges in the break room, brief conversations at company events—all meticulously cataloged and analyzed. From the security cameras? That was just creepy! Dan couldn't have meant for the app to access security footage. This information couldn't wait for the next meeting. Except it had to. She couldn't bring this matter to Dan's attention without revealing more of herself than she cared to. But she couldn't just let the app do this to some unsuspecting end user. *I'll just wait. If this happened to me, it'll happen again to somebody else.* She paused, frowning. *Wouldn't it? If it doesn't, I'll bring it up. Later.*

She was still working through her churning emotions when the app finished compiling its new gallery of photos, complete with a generative AI narrative highlighting the frequency of her interactions with Dan. Worse yet, using facial recognition, the app speculated on the pair's emotions, punctuating everything with a note: "Potential romantic interest detected." *Can apps smirk?*

Scarlett felt her cheeks burn. She glanced over at Dan, engrossed in his work and oblivious to her discovery.

Apparently catching her staring in his periphery, Dan looked up. "Everything okay?" he asked, concern evident in his voice.

"Yeah." Scarlett nodded quickly and minimized the ChronicleMe window. "Just... reviewing some work."

Dan's face lit up. "And?"

Scarlett gave him an awkward cross between a nod and a shrug, but before she could answer, Diego rounded a corner, his usual exuberance tempered by an undercurrent of nervousness.

"Guess who's officially part of the team?" he announced, waving a piece of paper. "HR just approved it!"

Surprised enough on her own, Scarlett watched Zoe's face turn pale, her knuckles whitening as she gripped her desk.

Dan got up and offered his hand. "That's... great, Diego. Welcome aboard."

As the two men chatted about it and laughed, Zoe scooted her chair close to her desk and leaned into her work, tension practically radiating from her.

The ChronicleMe window blinked on Scarlett's screen. She glanced over at Dan then looked at her screen again. *I don't care how intelligent you are. You're still artificial. You can't understand me or my feelings. How could you? Even I don't understand them.*

With a quick shake of her head, she banished the thought. *It's just a project—an intense one, but still. This whole thing with Dan is just... normal. When people work together and have zero social life...* Scarlett sighed. *Things just get out of proportion. If it looks like we're*

*spending a lot of time together, it's just that we're work-
ing. It'll all blow over after the launch.*

She took a deep breath. *I just need to focus. Everything else can wait.*

THE CHRONICLEME TEAM fell into a rhythm,
with each member focusing on their tasks. Scarlett's
renewed focus paid off. If she had to duck around
corners now and then to avoid getting caught on camera
with Dan, the results were worth the effort. Her
creative output took off. She felt especially productive
one morning after sharing her progress with the team.
Everyone loved her concept and how seamlessly it
flowed in the app. She hadn't experienced anything like
this since college, when praise seemed to fall in her lap.

As the meeting drew to a close, Zoe's eyes lit up.
"Hey, guys," she said, her voice brimming with excitement. "I've been thinking."

Diego's eyes sparkled as he gave her two thumbs up.
"Good job thinking, Zoe!"

Zoe narrowed her eyes then turned back to the
team. "You know, the marketing plan doesn't mention
social media, which seems kind of odd, since our app is
pretty much based on that. So anyway, I was thinking
we should start building some buzz about
ChronicleMe."

Dan raised his eyebrows and nodded. "Absolutely.
But we're a long way from sharing any of this publicly."

Zoe replied with a nod of her own. "I know, I know.

But hear me out. What if we start sharing little teasers on social media? Nothing that gives away what we're actually working on, just enough to pique people's curiosity. We'll call it the Mystery Project. Who doesn't love a mystery?"

Scarlett, who had been quietly sketching in her notebook, looked up. "That could be interesting. But how do we do that without revealing too much?"

"Easy." Zoe grinned. "We focus on the process, not the product. Behind-the-scenes stuff, you know? Like, pics of our whiteboard covered in sticky notes, Diego dozing, slack-jawed at the conference room table with drool on his chin."

"That was one time!" Diego protested.

Zoe's eyes twinkled as she continued. "Or a time-lapse video of us working late into the night. You know —sprawled around a table, empty Chinese food containers and soda cans strewn about—funny captions, zany antics... All the while, we'll be building anticipation, and all without giving anything away."

Diego nodded approvingly. "I like it. It's got that whole exclusive insider/reality show vibe. People eat that stuff up."

Dan considered for a moment then shrugged. "Okay. I'll run it by Max."

Zoe clapped her hands together. "I'll be our social media guru!"

Dan held up a hand. "But nothing gets posted without running it by me—and maybe Max."

Again, Zoe nodded. "Absolutely."

Over the next few weeks, Zoe's plan took shape. She posted carefully curated photos, first on her personal social media accounts then linking and transitioning them to new ChronicleMe accounts. The images included a blurred shot of code on a computer screen with the caption "Working on something big #StayTuned," a picture of the team huddled around a table of takeout containers with the caption "Late nights and big dreams #ComingSoon," and even a close-up of Scarlett's hand sketching an abstract design with the caption "#Beautyinthedetails #WatchThisSpace."

The posts gained traction, prompting threads from followers speculating wildly about what the team could be working on. The energy was palpable, giving the team a renewed sense of purpose.

Meanwhile, Dan's project drew attention from higher-ups in the company. One afternoon, the CEO and other executives called him into a meeting.

When he returned, his face flushed with excitement, he announced an impromptu meeting for the team. Once they'd assembled in the conference room, Dan cleared his throat. "I have an announcement. Max loves the idea of promoting ChronicleMe on social media." He paused, noticing Zoe's excited expression. "It was genius, Zoe." But his weak smile faded. "So... Max has brought in someone from corporate PR to take the lead."

Seeing Zoe's stunned look, Scarlett reached over and squeezed her hand.

As if on cue, a tall woman with impeccably styled blond hair and a crisp navy suit strode into the room.

"Everyone, this is Victoria Hawthorne from corporate PR," Dan announced, his tone neutral. "She'll be overseeing our progress."

Victoria's smile was dazzling, but it didn't quite reach her eyes. She strode to the front of the room, iPad in hand and confidence radiating off her like a spotlight. As VP, her reputation for balancing corporate priorities with ruthless efficiency preceded her. "All right, team," she said, scanning the group. "This project is under a microscope, so I'm here to make sure we do everything right and then make sure everyone knows it. Dan, Scarlett, I'll need updates by Friday. We'll talk more soon." After brief introductions, Victoria said a few more words in corporate speak then excused herself so she could hit the ground running.

After casting a farewell smile her way, Dan turned to the team. "Guys, you won't believe this. They want to feature ChronicleMe at the next company town hall. They're even talking about fast-tracking our launch!"

As cheers erupted from the team, Zoe muttered to Scarlett, "I wish they'd fast-track our lunch. Make mine liquid."

Scarlett smiled sympathetically then forced a smile in Dan's direction. She was happy for him, honestly, but she couldn't help feeling resentful on Zoe's behalf—and maybe a little envious on her own. Although he deserved to be lauded for his brilliant algorithm, where would it be without her visual design?

THE DAY of the town hall arrived, and the entire company gathered in the large auditorium. Dan was called to the stage, where he was presented with the company's Innovation Award for his work on ChronicleMe. As he accepted the award, he spoke passionately about the project and its potential to change how people interacted with their digital lives.

Scarlett watched from the audience with mixed emotions. Beside her, Zoe sank into her seat, arms folded. Next to Zoe, Diego leaned back in his usual manspread position, oblivious to anyone around him. At some point, Dan acknowledged the team, which was enough. It was more than enough. And yet, Scarlett couldn't help feeling left behind. She reminded herself it wasn't all about her. She was part of a team. As if punctuating that thought, the room burst into applause.

While the applause died down and people filed out, Scarlett slipped away for a moment alone. Outside, she drew in the fresh air and felt the world quietly settle back into proportion.

"Hey," Zoe said softly, joining her at the railing. "You okay?"

Scarlett shrugged. "Yeah, I'm fine. How about you?"

Zoe shrugged. "Fine." She narrowed her eyes. "What are you doing out here?"

Scarlett gave her head a slight shake. "Just… thinking."

Zoe nudged her gently. "There's thinking, and there's thinking. And I know that look."

Scarlett sighed. "It's stupid. I'm happy for Dan. It's just... I feel kind of... invisible."

Zoe's eyebrows drew together. "Your work is, kind of by definition, the most visible of anyone's."

Scarlett couldn't help but smile, but her expression faded too quickly. "Dan makes the magic, and I make the pretty."

"And I make the fun. I mean, they loved my social media campaign idea so much they took it away from me."

Scarlett pouted. "I know. That was just wrong." In silence, the two of them stared at the bustling city below for a few moments. "Dan deserves every bit of success." She glanced at Zoe. "This is really about me being disappointed in myself."

"For what?"

"I had so much potential, but I never achieved it."

Zoe raised her chin and peered at her friend. "You're not done yet, are you?"

"Well, no."

"So, life is a journey."

Scarlett winced. "Are you working a side hustle, writing motivational slogans?"

Zoe's eyes widened. "We could start our own poster business! You do the art, and I'll write the slogans. We'd kick that 'Hang in There' cat's butt!"

Smiling, Scarlett replied, "We don't need no stinkin' Town Hall award."

"Nope. We've got each other!"

They laughed for a moment, but in the next, they were serious.

"We have." Once more, Scarlett smiled.

Zoe forced a toothy grin. "And we've got ChronicleMe!"

"Yeah." Scarlett raised an eyebrow. "Do you ever wonder how you wound up here?"

With a nonchalant shrug, Zoe said, "I was just a simple girl with a dream. A bad dream." She added, "Just the Diego part. To be honest, it's a pretty sweet gig."

Scarlett had to agree. "It is. It's a great career—worth dreaming of."

Zoe said softly, "It just wasn't your dream."

Scarlett watched the cars driving along. "I do feel sometimes like I walked into somebody else's dream and got lost." She released a bitter chuckle. "There's probably some poor person out there wondering, 'What am I doing in this friggin' art gallery?'"

Zoe put an arm around her friend's shoulders. "You know what I think?"

That ever-positive outlook of Zoe's made Scarlett smile. "I feel another poster caption coming on," she said.

Zoe grinned. "Life is full of wrong turns in the road, and there's no 'Life GPS.'"

Scarlett squinted and stared into the distance. "That one might need some work."

Zoe started to laugh but turned and caught sight of Diego as he paused at the doorway, a conflicted expression on his face. His eyes darted toward Scarlett, then he turned and went on his way.

As Zoe watched him walk away, Scarlett said, "He doesn't know what he's missing."

"Oh, I think he does." Zoe let out a bitter chuckle of her won then turned back to Scarlett. "But Dan is another story."

"Dan?" Scarlett began to deny it, but Zoe gave her that knowing look that always disarmed her.

"Girl, don't even try to deny that you like him."

"Yeah, well..." Scarlett rolled her eyes and smirked. *Well, what? So I've got a work crush. Those don't mean anything.*

Then Zoe let out a loud gasp.

Startled, Scarlett cried, "What?"

"I just figured it out!"

"Figured what out?"

"You! None of this was about work. It's Dan! The attention you're craving—"

"*Craving's* a pretty strong word."

Zoe nodded. "My first thought was lust, but I didn't think you were ready to admit it."

Scarlett stood silent and slack-jawed.

Undeterred, Zoe continued. "It's okay. It's a phase. You know, when you don't want to admit you have feelings for... reasons. So your brain does a kind of denial-of-service signal to your heart. Just like with a cyber-attack, the two sides battle it out until the hack or antivirus—guys being the virus—wins out."

For a moment, Scarlett studied her friend. "You've really given this theory some thought."

Zoe laughed. "No, not really. It just came to me watching you and Dan exchange googly eyes."

"What? No." Scarlett looked away, shaking her head. "Googly eyes?" She started to roll her eyes again but stopped. "Wait, Dan too?"

Zoe answered with a knowing nod.

When the office had emptied hours later, Diego happened upon Zoe. At least, that was how it seemed. But Zoe knew Diego too well not to see through his tactics. They'd carefully avoided one-on-one interactions since he'd joined the team.

"So," Diego said, plopping down on Scarlett's vacated chair and wheeling over to Zoe. "This is... weird, huh?"

"You're weird. I'm working." Zoe answered, continuing to focus on her computer.

Diego flashed that grin with his bright white teeth and dark eyes. Not that Zoe saw it. She just knew it was there. She'd already made that mistake once. She wouldn't make it again.

Diego gestured between himself and Zoe. "Us working together again. Who thought that would ever happen?"

"Not me." Zoe sighed and leaned back in her chair, practically glaring.

Diego's eyes darted away.

She suppressed a satisfied smile. *Good. Squirm a little.*

Then he took her by surprise and looked honestly at her. "It's good to see you."

Her eyebrow shot up. "Yeah? Well, I'll be here all week. Try the veal."

He flinched. The reaction was barely perceptible, but it was there.

Inwardly, Zoe smiled.

"Look, Zo, I've wanted to tell you, but there's never a good time." He glanced around at the now-empty office. "This place is intense—not like the old start-up days. This place is buzzing, and you always look so busy."

"Because I am."

He ran his hand through his coarse black hair. "This isn't coming out like I wanted." He leaned forward, his elbows on his knees. "Zo, I'm sorry. For everything. I know I messed up, big time."

Despite the many times as she'd imagined a conversation like this, she didn't feel nearly as victorious as she'd expected. She just felt tired—too tired to be sad. "Yeah, you did."

Gone was Diego's usual blustering voice. "I was scared... of commitment, of settling down, of... of how much I cared about you."

Now came Zoe's turn to flinch. A rush of emotion she thought she'd been rid of came to the surface. It didn't help to see sorrow—sincere sorrow—in Diego's eyes. Those deep brown eyes with that rare, soft look that always did her in.

"So, I ran. It was stupid and cowardly, and I've regretted it every day since."

Zoe was quiet for a moment, processing his words. "I guess we all have regrets." *Like ever being with you.*

Diego's fingers twitched, almost touched her knee, and withdrew. "Because... because I think you deserve to know. And because working with you again, seeing you every day... It's made me realize even more how much... how much I miss you... and how much I still..." He swallowed, unable to finish the sentence.

Zoe's eyes widened as she realized what he was trying to say. "Don't," she said softly. She couldn't seem to stop shaking her head. "We're not... I'm not going through that again."

Diego nodded, a mix of sadness and understanding on his face. "I know. I'm not..." He heaved a sigh. "I just... needed to say it—so you'd know."

And what good does that do—other than ease your conscience and dump your burden on me? They sat in silence, the weight of their history hanging between them.

Finally, Zoe spoke. "Look, we're both professionals. We can work together on this project without letting the past get in the way. We've done it so far, haven't we?"

Diego managed a small smile. "Right. Absolutely. Just colleagues."

He hesitated then got up and walked back to his desk.

THE NEXT DAY, Scarlett arrived at the office early, her mind buzzing with ideas. She had spent most of the night sketching, trying to channel her frustrations into something productive. As she settled at her desk and opened her design software, something clicked in her mind.

"That's it," she muttered, her fingers flying across the keyboard. "That's what's been missing."

Hours passed in a blur of creativity. When Dan arrived, he found Scarlett surrounded by printouts and digital mockups, her eyes bright with excitement.

"Scarlett?" he said, approaching her cautiously. "You okay?"

She looked up, a wide grin spreading across her face. "Dan, I've got it. I know how to make ChronicleMe not just functional but beautiful. Look."

She pulled him over to her computer, where she explained her vision and made animated gestures throughout. Dan listened, his eyes growing wider with each passing moment.

"Scarlett, this is... This is incredible," he said when she finished. "It's exactly what we needed. It's next-level."

Scarlett beamed, feeling the old surge of pride she thought she'd lost.

As word of Scarlett's breakthrough spread, the energy in the office reached new heights. Even Diego, who had been somewhat on the periphery of the project, was caught up in the excitement.

During the team's next meeting with the executives, as others presented their progress, Diego chimed in with suggestions and ideas, his natural charm on full display.

Once they began filing out of the conference room, Zoe pulled Diego aside. "What was that?" she hissed.

Diego held up his hands defensively. "What? I was just trying to help."

Zoe narrowed her eyes. "You used your Diego charm to weasel your way into their good graces."

"Is that such a bad thing?" he asked, a hint of his old mischievous smile playing on his lips. "There's more to me than just this handsome face."

Zoe rolled her eyes, but Diego could swear he saw the ghost of a smile tugging at the corners of her mouth. "Just... don't mess up this project, okay?" she asked. "It means a lot to us all."

His expression softened. "I know."

8

T he late afternoon sun cast long shadows across the office as Dan, Scarlett, Zoe, and Diego huddled around Dan's desk. The air was thick with anticipation and the lingering smell of pizza.

"All right," Dan said, his fingers hovering over the keyboard. "This is it. The moment of truth."

Perched on the edge of the desk, Zoe nodded excitedly. "I can't believe we're finally here. Who's going first?"

Dan grinned at Zoe. "How 'bout you?"

Zoe clapped her hands together, her eyes sparkling with excitement. "Me? Oh, I'm so ready for this!"

She leaned forward, practically bouncing on her toes as Dan input her information into ChronicleMe. The room fell silent, save for the soft clicking of keys and the hum of the computer.

Suddenly, the screen burst to life with a vibrant display of colors and images. A lively melody began to play as a smooth, engaging AI-generated voice started narrating Zoe's life story.

"Whoa!" Diego exclaimed, leaning in closer. "This is like a mini movie!"

The presentation unfolded in a dazzling montage of snapshots and photos, each one seamlessly transitioning into the next. Moments from Zoe's childhood, college years, and recent adventures flashed across the screen, accompanied by animated graphics that seemed to dance around the images.

"The graphics are incredible," Dan said, filled with admiration. "Scarlett, you designed all of this?"

Scarlett's eyes shone. "Oh, it's just some preliminary ideas. It's a work in progress."

Still overwhelmed, Dan gazed at Scarlett. His heart swelled with admiration. "Preliminary? This is amazing work."

Diego, sprawled in a nearby chair, caught Dan staring at Scarlett and gave him an unsubtle elbow to the ribs as a knowing grin spread across his face.

Dan blinked and abruptly turned back to the screen, frowning.

Zoe, apparently oblivious to the exchange, was completely engrossed in her digital life story. "Oh my gosh, I forgot about that trip to Yosemite! And look at my hair in college!" She laughed, pointing at a particularly awkward photo. "This is incredible, you guys. It's like reliving my whole life in the most beautiful way possible."

Once the presentation came to an end, set to a

crescendo of uplifting music, the team sat in stunned silence for a moment.

"Well," Diego said finally, breaking the spell, "I think it's safe to say that was a success. Who's next?" When no one spoke up, Diego grinned. "I vote for Dan. It's his baby, after all."

Scarlett, standing close to Dan with her arms crossed, looked less confident. "I don't think we ran a simulation on this."

Dan shook his head. "We've done all the simulations we'd planned." He glanced around at his team. "But Scarlett's right—we should choose randomly. It's only fair."

Zoe rummaged in her desk drawer, retrieved three strips of paper from it, and cut them. "Here," she said, holding them out. "Short one goes first."

They each drew a paper, and Dan unfolded his hand to reveal the shortest one. He let out a nervous chuckle. "It must be destiny."

With a deep breath, Dan entered his credentials into ChronicleMe. The screen flickered for a moment then burst into a vibrant timeline of Dan's digital life.

"Wow," Zoe breathed. "It's beautiful. The interface is perfect, Scarlett."

Scarlett smiled softly, feeling proud but still nervous. For the first time, most of the team was seeing the full effect of her work.

Dan's timeline looked ideal. The app had accurately pieced together Dan's work history, his hobbies, and even his favorite coffee shop.

As the team huddled around Dan's computer, Scarlett was acutely aware of his presence next to her. The warmth of his arm against hers, the faint scent of his cologne—the effect was distracting in a way she wasn't prepared for.

But as they neared the present day, the unexpected appeared. A series of photos and posts, algorithmically paired with a romantic ballad, suggested a budding romance between Dan and Scarlett. There were photos of them in the office, leaning on Scarlett's car, chatting, and individual shots of them on the phone spliced together to imply they were talking to each other. Then it got strange. The AI seemed to have fabricated dinner dates, movie nights—even a weekend getaway that looked alarmingly real but had never happened.

The room fell silent. Scarlett's face flushed a deep red, and Dan stared at the screen in disbelief. She stole a glance at Dan, only to find him already looking at her, his eyes unreadable.

For a moment, the air between the two of them seemed charged with alarm and discomfort. Then Dan cleared his throat, breaking the spell. "It's just an AI hallucination," he said, but Scarlett couldn't help noticing the slight tremor in his voice.

Diego was the first to shatter the silence with a low whistle. "Well, well, well. Looks like someone's been holding out on us."

"This... this isn't right," Dan stammered. "These events never happened."

Diego grinned and raised an eyebrow.

Ignoring him, Dan said, "I thought we'd built in enough model-specific preemptive hallucination detection. While we work on that, we can fine-tune the prompt engineering." As Dan explained the issue and assigned tasks to solve it, Scarlett wondered if the app had detected something they'd both been ignoring.

Zoe leaned in more closely to the computer, her brow furrowed. "But the app is supposed to only use real data. How could it fabricate all this?"

Scarlett, her voice barely above a whisper, added, "Not just how. Why?"

Dan ran a hand through his hair and glanced about. "It's misinterpreting the photos."

Diego raised an eyebrow. "Or something in them." His eyes twinkled. "Or maybe it's picking up on something you two are too blind to see."

"Diego." Zoe gave his ankle a kick.

Now red-faced, Dan closed his laptop. "It's a work in progress. Just a bump in the road."

Scarlett nodded, not meeting anyone's eyes. "I should... I should go. It's late. We can tackle this fresh in the morning."

As Scarlett gathered her belongings and hurried out, Dan called after her, "Scarlett, wait—" But she was already gone.

The remaining three sat briefly in awkward silence before Diego stood up. "Well, that was... interesting. I think I'll head out too. Good luck with that bug, Dan."

After Diego left, Zoe turned to Dan, her expression a mix of concern and curiosity. "Dan, are you okay?"

Dan nodded absently, his eyes still fixed on the now-blank screen. "Yeah, I'm fine. Just a minor setback. We'll figure it out."

As Zoe said goodnight and left, Dan opened the program again. He stared at the fabricated timeline of his nonexistent relationship with Scarlett. With a sigh, he began to comb through the code, determined to find a way to fix this mess.

But deep down, a small part of him wondered if the app had simply revealed a truth he wasn't ready to face.

IN THE PRE-DAWN HOURS, the office was eerily quiet as Scarlett worked her way through the maze of cubicles. The app's bizarre prediction had replayed in her mind until, unable to sleep, she gave up and returned to work. Figuring the office would be empty, with nothing to distract her, she looked forward to getting some work done.

She rounded the corner and stopped. From Dan's desk, a faint blue glow bathed his face in soft light as he hunched over his keyboard.

Startled, he turned. "Scarlett!" He glanced at his watch.

Feeling self-conscious, she shrugged. "I couldn't sleep."

Dan ran a hand through his disheveled hair. "Me neither. Look, I'm sorry... about earlier."

Scarlett felt suddenly uncomfortable discussing the matter. "Like you said. AI hallucination." She shrugged as if it meant nothing, which wasn't even close to the truth. Desperate to change the subject, she noticed the dark circles under his eyes and the empty coffee cups littering his desk. "Have you been here all night?"

He nodded, stifling a yawn. "Yeah. I need to fix this."

"From the looks of it, you need to sleep."

He shook his head stubbornly. "Speak for yourself. I can't. This app's too important. I can't let it fail."

Something in his voice and the strain in his red-rimmed eyes made Scarlett pause. "Why?"

He averted his eyes. "What do you mean, why? It's a big project."

"I know that." She pulled up a chair and sat beside him. "But really, why? In the end, isn't it just another app?"

"Yeah. And it's my career." Dan was quiet for a long while as he absently ran his fingers over his watch face.

Something about his nervous gesture amused her. "You're going to wear that thing out."

To her surprise, he cast a serious and slightly unsettling look. Maybe she was misreading him, but, having had a few glimpses of the true man beneath the dispassionate businessman, she wondered if there wasn't something else going on besides work. He let go of his wrist and glanced down at his watch. "My sister gave this to me."

"Nice gift."

"It was."

With a nod toward the watch, Scarlett said, "Does that thing have an alarm? You could set it for 'time to go home and get some sleep.'"

He made a poor attempt at a laugh.

"Not that I'm one to talk." She gave him a self-deprecating smile. Perhaps her lack of sleep was at fault, but she felt uncharacteristically philosophical. "Why do you do it?"

The question seemed to catch him off guard. "Why? Because I enjoy it. I like getting paid, paying rent, eating pizza." He grinned, but it faded, and a dark look replaced the expression.

With a deep sigh, he turned to face her. "My sister, Mandy," he began, his voice barely above a whisper. "She... died two years ago."

Scarlett's heart clenched. "Oh, Dan. I'm so sorry."

He nodded, swallowing hard. "It was an accident. She was pulling an all-nighter for finals and took some Adderall, and it was laced with fentanyl."

Scarlett instinctively reached out and placed her hand over his. Dan looked down at their hands then back up at her, his eyes shimmering with unshed tears.

"After she died, we found her journals. They were full of these beautiful, funny, heartbreaking stories about her life. Things we never knew." His voice cracked. "It was sad and, at the same time, uplifting. It felt good to see a full picture of the Mandy we loved. And I thought of how lucky we were. If only everyone had a way to remember their loved ones like that... And then extensions of that—other uses—came to mind. The ideas kept coming. I couldn't let them go.

"And ChronicleMe was born."

"That's..." Their eyes met, and Scarlett lost herself in his gaze. "... beautiful."

He looked away. "But now... after last night... I'm

wondering if I've created something that could hurt people more than it helps. What if it reveals things they're not ready to face, let alone share?"

Scarlett felt a surge of emotions—admiration for Dan's vision, sorrow for his loss, and a deep desire to comfort him. Without thinking, she reached out and gripped his shoulder. "Dan, you'll fix this," she said, her voice soft but firm. "What you've created is amazing."

He cast a doubtful look at her.

Undeterred, she persisted. "So, there's a bug, but we'll fix it."

He shook his head, looking defeated. "Seven hours ago, I would've agreed. But I've been at this for hours, and I can't—"

"But you will!"

Dan stared at her, a mix of gratitude and something else—something deeper—in his eyes. "How do you do that?" he whispered.

"Do what?"

"See the best in things. In people. Even when they're being stubborn workaholics."

"It's a gift. And a curse. Especially when dealing with stubborn workaholics." Scarlett smiled.

Dan smiled back—a genuine smile that reached his eyes and made Scarlett's heart skip a beat. For a moment, her eyes locked with his, Scarlett thought they might kiss. Their lips parted, her heart pounded, and the world seemed to stop.

The whir of a floor polisher broke through the stillness, and the moment evaporated.

Dan stood up and gently pulled Scarlett to her feet. "Come here. I want to show you something."

Confused but intrigued, Scarlett followed him to the elevator. They rode in comfortable silence to the top floor then climbed a short flight of stairs. Dan pushed open a door, and they stepped out onto the roof.

Scarlett gasped. The city stretched out before them, a glittering tapestry of lights under a velvet sky studded with stars. A cool breeze carried the faint scent of jasmine from the garden below.

"Wow," Scarlett whispered.

Smiling, Dan led her to the rail at the edge of the roof. "I come up here sometimes when I need to clear my head. To remind myself that there's a whole world out there beyond codes and algorithms."

Under the starlit sky, Dan's usual defenses seemed to crumble. "Sometimes I wonder if I'm doing the right thing," he confessed, his voice barely above a whisper. "What if I've created a monster—albeit a technical one?"

Scarlett felt an overwhelming urge to comfort him, but after what they'd just seen, she held back. "Dan, look at me," she said softly. "What you're creating... it's incredible. It has the power to help people understand themselves, to connect with others in ways they never could before."

Dan's eyes met hers again, vulnerability clear in his gaze. "How can you be so sure?"

"Because I've seen it," Scarlett replied, surprising herself with her conviction. "I've seen how it's changed the way I think about my own life, my own connections. And that's just the beginning."

"Or the end—if I can't figure out what just happened in there."

Her eyes flitted toward him, but she couldn't meet them. "Yeah, well... that's just a little bump in the road."

He raised an eyebrow, and they both smiled.

But as Scarlett gazed into his warm hazel eyes, the lines dividing the categories of colleague, friend, and something more blurred, and for once, she wasn't sure she wanted to redraw them. In the moonlight, she saw not just the brilliant programmer but a man with passion, kindness, and pain—a man who truly wanted to make the world better.

"It's going to happen," she said softly. "You're going to make it happen." A breeze tossed strands of her hair on her face.

Without warning, Dan reached out and tucked the stray hair behind Scarlett's ear. His hand lingered and gently cupped her cheek. Her breath caught in her throat.

"Scarlett," Dan murmured, "I think ChronicleMe was right."

"About?" she whispered, her heart pounding.

"This," Dan said. He leaned in and pressed his lips to hers.

The kiss was soft at first, tentative, but quickly deepened as Scarlett responded. She wound her arms around his neck as his hands found her waist and pulled her closer. The world seemed to fall away, leaving only the two of them under the vast, star-filled sky.

When they finally broke apart, both nearly breathless, Scarlett rested her forehead against Dan's.

"Wow," she said softly.

Dan chuckled. "Yeah. Wow."

They stood there for a long while, holding each other, the city lights twinkling below them.

Dan took a step back and glanced up at a security camera. "Let's not give the app footage for Episode Two."

Scarlett shut her eyes and exhaled. "Right. The app. We need to fix that tomorrow."

As they stepped into the elevator, Dan slipped his hand into Scarlett's. "Screw the app." Then he drew her to him and kissed her all the way down to the ground floor.

9

The aroma of freshly brewed coffee filled the company cafe as Scarlett stirred her latte, watching the foam swirl into intricate patterns. Across the table, Zoe sipped her triple-shot espresso, her eyes twinkling with curiosity.

"Okay, spill," Zoe said, setting down her cup. "You've been acting weird all morning. What's up?"

Scarlett felt a blush creep up her neck. "Is it that obvious?"

Zoe rolled her eyes good-naturedly. "Only to someone who's known you for years. Come on, what's going on?"

After taking a deep breath, Scarlett leaned in closer and whispered, "It's... Dan."

Zoe's eyebrows shot up. "Dan? Our Dan? Mr. 'I live and breathe code' Dan?"

Scarlett nodded, a small smile playing on her lips. "I know it sounds crazy, but... I think I've misjudged him." She looked down. "He's different."

Zoe eyed her suspiciously. "Really?"

Scarlett tried to look nonchalant. "Apparently, he's not the annoying tech bro I thought he was."

"Oh?" Zoe leaned in, intrigued. "That sounds like a story. Let's hear it."

"Well," Scarlett began, choosing her words carefully, "there's nothing to tell, really. It's just... we've been working closely—"

Again, Zoe's eyes twinkled. "Closely? Mm-hmm. Go on."

Scarlett shook her head. "That's it. I've seen a different side of him, is all. He's passionate—"

Zoe raised an eyebrow.

"And... kind of sweet, actually. Stop it!"

"Stop what?"

Scarlett pointed at Zoe's widening grin. "That!"

Zoe bit her lips, which seemed only to brighten the amused look in her eyes. "Kind of sweet, huh? Sounds like someone's got a crush."

Scarlett's cheeks burned. "No. It's not... I mean, I wouldn't call it a crush." The feeling of his lips on hers flashed through her mind. "It's—it's just... different."

"Good different or bad different?"

"Definitely good!" Scarlett realized she might have said that too loudly. "I feel like I'm seeing the real Dan, you know? Beyond that coding genius facade, he's actually got a nice—"

"Butt?"

"Personality," Scarlett corrected.

Zoe giggled and made air quotes. "A nice firm... 'personality.'"

Now it was Scarlett who rolled her eyes. "Why did I even bother to tell you?"

"Because if you didn't tell someone, you'd explode."

Scarlett gave up trying to hide how she felt. "Probably."

Zoe leaned forward. "Let me get this straight. So, he knows how you feel."

Scarlett nodded.

"And he feels the same way?"

Scarlett nodded again.

Zoe stared straight into her eyes. "And you know this because he told you... with his lips?"

Scarlett laughed. "Zoe, do you have to make it sound like—"

"He kissed you? Well, yeah, because he obviously did."

Scarlett exhaled and admitted, "He did."

Now Zoe's expression softened. "I'm glad. It's nice when two people I like... surprise each other like that."

Something in Zoe's tone made Scarlett pause. "Speaking of surprises, how are things with Diego?"

It was Zoe's turn to blush. "Actually, I've been meaning to talk to you about that. I've had my own change of heart. Maybe! I mean... he's got some convincing to do, but... he's been different."

"Really?" Scarlett was stunned.

With a hint of vulnerability in her eyes, Zoe nodded.

The last time they discussed the matter, Zoe was adamant about keeping her distance from Diego. Who could blame her? He'd broken her heart.

Zoe shook her head. "I know what you're thinking."

"I'm not thinking anything except what you've told me—how deeply he hurt you."

Zoe's eyebrows drew together. "I know. And I haven't forgotten. Believe me! But he's been different lately. More mature, I guess. I mean, people can change, can't they? We've had a few good conversations, and I'm beginning to think that maybe—"

She stopped abruptly and stared out the window. Scarlett followed her line of sight and then felt her heart sink. Outside, Diego was stepping out of a sleek black car, followed closely by Victoria Hawthorne, the social media guru from PR. They were laughing about something, and Victoria's hand lingered on Diego's arm for a moment too long for the gesture to be purely professional.

"Oh," Scarlett said softly.

"Wow." Zoe's face had hardened, her earlier vulnerability replaced by a mask of stunned impassivity. "I'm an idiot," she said, her voice tight.

Scarlett leaned forward. "No! You are anything but! You're a wonderful, caring, and generous woman!"

With her eyes fixed on Diego and Victoria as they entered the building, Zoe barely reacted.

Scarlett urged Zoe, "Don't jump to conclusions. Maybe it's not what it looks like."

Zoe managed a weak laugh. "With Diego, it's always just what it looks like."

An hour later, the team gathered in the conference room for their daily standup. Victoria stood at the head of the table, her tablet in hand and a self-satisfied smile on her face. Scarlett couldn't help but notice how Victoria's gaze lingered on Diego while he entered the room, her smile widening almost imperceptibly.

Diego, for his part, seemed to bask in the attention. He flashed Victoria a quick wink as he took a seat beside Zoe, oblivious to the way Zoe stiffened. Scarlett felt a pang of sympathy for her friend, who was clearly trying to maintain an indifferent facade.

As Dan entered the room, his eyes met Scarlett's, and she felt a flutter in her stomach. Their shared moment on the rooftop last night seemed to hover between them, unspoken but palpable. Dan offered her a small, private smile before taking his seat.

Max slipped in unexpectedly at the last minute and took a seat of her own. Seeing her, Dan leaned over to Scarlett and said softly, "Be ready. I'm going to ask you to walk us through your portion. They need to see what you've done." With an encouraging smile, he turned his attention to Victoria.

"Good morning, everyone," Victoria began. "Let's start with a demonstration of where we are with the app. Dan?"

"Sure." He walked them through a slide highlighting the progress he and his teammates had made as well as some challenges they were working through. Then he glanced at Scarlett. "Let's dive into the visuals," Dan said, nodding toward her. "This is Scarlett's area."

Scarlett tamped down a surge of panic and then squared her shoulders and stood.

"Thanks, Dan," she said, projecting more confidence than she felt. Clicking on the first slide, she launched into her presentation.

"Our goal with ChronicleMe was to move beyond functionality and create an emotional connection. These visuals are designed to guide users through their narratives, making every interaction intuitive and meaningful. To that end, the background colors and shapes are keyed into the text and images to enhance the emotional resonance."

As she spoke, she outlined an assortment of color schemes, layouts, and animations she'd developed, tying each choice to user engagement and emotional impact.

Victoria leaned forward, scrutinizing the slides. "And how does this scale? Have you considered broader applications?"

Scarlett met her gaze, refusing to falter. "Yes. Every element is optimized for scalability and flexibility. The core design ensures that the app remains seamless across all devices, even as we expand features while digging down to more granular levels."

The room was quiet as the presentation ended, but murmurs of approval quickly followed. Diego said, "This takes ChronicleMe to a whole new level."

Even Victoria gave a begrudging nod. "It's a strong start. Let's see if the implementation holds up."

As the meeting wrapped up, Dan caught Scarlett's eye. "Good work," he said, his voice quieter than usual but his tone unmistakably sincere.

Max, who had observed the presentation from the back, approached Dan and Scarlett on her way out and asked them to step outside. "Dan, this is impressive. And Scarlett, when the time comes, I want you to co-present this to the board. Your designs are beautiful, of course, but the way you've explained your vision, your process in implementing it, and how it ultimately functions send it over the finish line. The board needs to see this firsthand."

As Max headed for her office, Scarlett stared at Dan with saucer eyes, unsure of what to say.

Dan grinned. "Wow! Good for you."

"Really?"

He made a face as though she were nuts. "Of course, really."

Scarlett glanced inside the room, where the meeting continued. "I just... I don't want you to think I was trying to steal your thunder."

Dan rolled his eyes. "I asked you to speak so they'd see your work the way I see it—the way everyone will see it. It's amazing. So stop fretting, and let's go back into the meeting."

Scarlett nodded, barely able to stop smiling as she returned to the conference room.

In a voice was brimming with enthusiasm, Victoria announced, "I have some exciting news about our social media campaign."

Scarlett glanced at Zoe, who was studiously avoiding looking at Diego. For his part, Diego seemed oblivious to the tension, focusing on Victoria. The way they interacted held an easy familiarity, suggesting their arrival together at work wasn't an isolated incident.

"The preliminary numbers are in," Victoria continued, her eyes sparkling with triumph, "and I'm thrilled to report that our campaign is already exceeding expectations. We've seen a five hundred percent increase in engagement across all platforms, and the hashtag ChronicleMeMagic is trending nationally."

A smattering of applause arose. Scarlett noticed that Dan remained silent, his brow furrowed. She could almost see the gears turning in his head. But he got that way whenever he hit a wall in the app's progress.

"But the real coup," Victoria said, her smile widening as she cast a conspiratorial glance at Diego, "is this article that just went live on *TechMunch*. Diego was instrumental in providing some of the background information that made this piece so... compelling."

At this information, Zoe's head snapped up. Her eyes narrowed as she looked between Diego and Victoria. Diego, sensing the sudden tension, had the good sense to look slightly uncomfortable.

As Victoria spoke, Zoe's thumbs flew across her phone screen. Suddenly, her eyes widened, and she let out a small gasp. With a pale face, she turned to Scarlett and wordlessly handed over her phone.

Scarlett looked down at the screen, and her stomach dropped as she read the headline: "ChronicleMe: The App Born from Tragedy—Exclusive Inside Look at Creator Dan Weston."

Before she could read further, Dan reached across the table. His hand brushed against Scarlett's. The brief contact sent a jolt through her, and she found herself momentarily distracted by the warmth of his skin.

"May I?" he asked, his voice tight.

Scarlett nodded, reluctantly handing him the phone.

Oblivious to the growing tension, Victoria continued her presentation. "This article is already generating significant buzz," she said, her voice almost gleeful. "The personal angle really resonates with readers, and we're seeing a surge in preregistrations for the app. People are connecting with the story on an emotional level."

As Victoria happily went on highlighting the article's success, Scarlett felt a knot form in her stomach. She glanced at Dan, seeing the color drain from his face as he scrolled through the article. His free hand, which had been resting on the table, curled into a fist, and Scarlett had to fight the urge to reach out and comfort him.

When Dan spoke, his voice was low and dangerous, cutting through Victoria's self-congratulatory monologue. "What is this?"

Victoria faltered for the first time, her perfectly crafted persona showing a crack. "I'm sorry?"

"This article," Dan said, his voice rising. The raw pain in his tone made Scarlett's heart ache. "Who authorized this?"

"I... I did," Victoria replied, her confidence apparently wavering. She glanced at Diego as if seeking backup, but he was suddenly very interested in his shoes. "It's a powerful story, Dan. It humanizes the app and gives it emotional weight. Diego mentioned your personal connection to the project, and we thought—"

"You thought?" Dan stood abruptly, his chair scraping loudly against the floor. Everyone flinched at the sudden movement. "That's my sister. My family's tragedy. You had no right to share that without my permission."

The room fell silent. Now the tension had become palpable. Victoria's perfectly composed facade cracked further, a flicker of fear crossing her face as she realized the magnitude of her miscalculation. "Dan, I... I thought you understood. This kind of personal connection is marketing gold. It's what will set ChronicleMe apart from other apps."

"Marketing gold?" Dan sounded incredulous, his voice laced with a fury Scarlett had never heard from him before. "Is that all my sister's death is to you? A marketing opportunity?"

Diego finally spoke up, his own voice uncharacteristically subdued. "Dan, man, I'm sorry. I didn't think—"

"No, you didn't think," Dan cut him off, his eyes flashing. "Neither of you did."

Before anyone else could respond, Dan turned and stormed out of the room. He slammed the door behind him.

No one moved. The deafening silence was broken only by the sound of Victoria's heels as she shifted uncomfortably. Scarlett felt torn between her desire to go after Dan and her duty to the team.

Finally, she stood. "I'll, uh... go check on him," she said, her voice shaky.

As she reached the door, she heard Victoria's voice behind her, strained but still trying to maintain control. "Well," the PR maven said, "I think we can all agree that Dan's reaction just proves how powerful this story is. That sort of raw emotion is exactly what will draw people to ChronicleMe."

Scarlett paused, her hand on the doorknob. She looked behind her and fixed Victoria with a cold stare that made the older woman lean back. "No, Victoria. What this proves is that you crossed a line. You exploited his pain."

"For the good of the project!" Victoria fired back in defense.

Scarlett shook her head slowly. "You've betrayed Dan's trust, violated his privacy, and potentially damaged the entire project."

"But isn't this what we wanted—behind-the-scenes human interest to build a buzz for the project?"

"This is exactly what we did not want," Scarlett found herself saying, her voice stronger than she expected. "We're supposed to uplift people, not exploit their personal stories for publicity."

Victoria regarded her quizzically. "It's just good marketing, Scarlett."

"No," Scarlett's eyes swept the room, taking in Diego's guilty expression, Zoe's blend of anger and hurt, and the shocked faces of the rest of the team. "All I see are a couple of people who forgot to be human."

With that, Scarlett left the room, her heart pounding, in search of Dan. The situation was about to become much more complicated. The project, the team dynamics, her budding feelings for Dan—everything seemed to be hanging by a thread.

She found Dan on the roof, in the same spot where they had shared their kiss the night before. He was standing at the edge, his hands gripping the railing so tightly that his knuckles were white. The sight of him, silhouetted against the city skyline and looking so vulnerable, made Scarlett ache.

"Dan?" she called softly, not wanting to startle him.

He turned, and the pain in his eyes nearly took her breath away. Without thinking, she crossed the distance between them and wrapped her arms around him. For a moment, he stood stiffly in her embrace, but then he seemed to crumble, his arms encircling her as he buried his face in her hair.

They stood like that for a long time, the city bustling below them, as Scarlett held Dan while he grieved for his sister, the invasion of his privacy, and the corruption of his dream. And as she held him, Scarlett made a silent vow to herself. She would help him fix this mess. Together, they would make ChronicleMe what it was meant to be—a tool for connection, under-standing, and healing. No matter what it took.

10

The tension in the conference room was palpable as the ChronicleMe team gathered for an emergency meeting. Scarlett's eyes darted among her colleagues, taking in their worried expressions. At the head of the table sat Dan, his face a mask of barely contained anger. Zoe kept glaring daggers at Diego, who looked like he wanted to sink into the floor. Victoria, for once, seemed to have lost her polished demeanor, fidgeting nervously with her tablet.

Dan cleared his throat, silencing the murmurs around the table. "I think we all know why we're here," he began, his voice tight with suppressed emotion. "The unauthorized article about my sister has put us in a... difficult position."

Victoria straightened in her chair and seemingly found her voice. "Dan, I want to apologize again. I truly thought—"

"Save it," Dan interrupted her, his tone icy. "The damage is done. Now we need to figure out how to move forward without compromising the integrity of ChronicleMe or anyone else's privacy—especially our potential users."

Zoe said quietly, "There have been some comments on social media." When Dan shot her a questioning look, she continued. "People are guessing the app's about dealing with tragedy and grief." She hesitated. "And... there are some privacy concerns."

Dan's expression grew even more pained. "The whole point was to celebrate life and connections." He shook his head and stared down at the table, clenching his jaw.

Her mind racing, Scarlett leaned forward. "So... we release a statement, something that addresses that—the joy of our fondest memories and the choice of how much or how little we share."

Dan raised his gaze to meet Scarlett's. "I get what you're saying, but I don't get how we do that without revealing the app's functionality prematurely."

Diego leaned in enthusiastically. "Maybe it's time to leak a little—just enough to emphasize how the user controls what they keep private."

Zoe scoffed, rolling her eyes. "Oh, now you care about privacy?"

Again, the room fell silent, and the tension ratcheted up another notch. Diego opened his mouth to respond, but Dan held up a hand, silencing him.

"Enough," Dan insisted. "We can't afford to be at each other's throats right now. Scarlett, can you draft a statement?"

"Don't you think that would be better done by a PR professional?" Victoria interjected.

Dan leveled a look that silenced the room. "I think we're ready for a different approach."

Victoria leaned back and folded her arms. "Let's see what Max has to say."

Scarlett and Zoe exchanged cautious expressions as Dan quietly said, "Do you really want to go there?"

Victoria's eyes widened just a bit, and then she smiled and said with syrupy warmth, "What I want is to give ChronicleMe the success it deserves."

"Good," Dan said sharply. "So, Scarlett, you draft a statement—something that reassures our potential users without revealing our hand to competitors."

Scarlett nodded, already mentally composing the message. "I'll have something for you to review within the hour."

"Good," Dan replied. His eyes softened as they met hers. "Zoe, keep tabs on social media and keep me apprised."

Zoe gave a curt nod.

"And Diego...?" Dan drew in a breath and softly exhaled. "Go over the app with a fine-toothed comb. Not only make sure every privacy protection is solid but tweak the filters to screen out negative items—firings, relationship break-ups, legal and criminal issues—everything that could possibly shed a negative light on the user experience."

Diego nodded solemnly. "You got it."

"And Victoria," Dan said, his tone cooling again as

he addressed the PR manager. "May I have a word? Everyone else can go."

Another heavy silence fell over the team as the meeting dispersed.

Minutes later, Scarlett stepped out of the restroom as Victoria stormed past. Scarlett stood and stared for a moment.

From behind her, Dan called out, "Scarlett, do you have a minute?"

"Sure." Her heart rate increased. Between last night's kiss and this morning's drama, everything had become too intense.

Dan said quietly, "Meet me on the roof," and continued on his way.

When Scarlett stepped out of the elevator, she found Dan in his favorite spot, leaning on the railing, looking out at the city.

With a deep sigh, he pushed back his hair. "What a friggin' mess," he said, his voice barely above a whisper.

Without thinking, Scarlett moved to his side. "Yeah." Her eyes met his, and seeing Dan's defeated expression, Scarlett brightened. "But it's only a setback. It's entirely fixable." *I hope.*

Dan studied her. "How do you do that?"

"Do what?"

"Lie so convincingly," he said, a smile tugging at his lips.

Scarlett couldn't suppress a broad smile of her own. "It's not a lie if we make it come true." She tried to ignore the butterflies that filled her stomach at the look in his eyes. He looked frustrated, lost, grateful, and thoroughly vulnerable. Time seemed to stop—like the moment before they might kiss.

But they didn't.

"So..." Scarlett took a breath. "About that statement..."

"Right. Let's go back and brainstorm some key points."

"Sure."

She turned away and took a step, but Dan grabbed her hand. "Wait." He seemed to be searching for words. "There's a lot going on."

"Yeah, there is!" Scarlett said with another smile.

Dan looked somber. "I'm still trying to take it all in. But..." He made a halfhearted shrug. "Thank you."

For what? Before Scarlett could get those words out, he drew her into his arms and held her.

Scarlett whispered, "It'll be okay."

Dan managed a smile. "There you go, lying again."

But as Scarlett gazed into his eyes, she felt certain. "It will."

With a light laugh, Dan said, "For now, let's go with that." Arm in arm, they walked back to the elevator and headed downstairs.

For the next hour, they worked side by side, crafting a statement that they hoped would reassure their potential users without revealing too much about the app.

As they huddled over Dan's computer, Scarlett was struck by how in sync they'd become. Finishing each other's sentences and building on each other's ideas, they completed the statement and high-fived one another.

"We make a good team," Dan said softly, his gaze lingering on hers.

Scarlett's heart skipped a beat. "Yeah," she replied, her voice equally soft. "We do."

Briefly, they just looked at each other, the air between them charged with unspoken emotions. When Scarlett was focused on a task, she could cope with the distraction of Dan's presence—the faint scent of his cologne, the warmth radiating from his body when he leaned close to look at her screen. But now, with the statement complete and that look in Dan's eyes, she wondered how she could be expected to work under such conditions.

Remembering where they were, Scarlett cleared her throat. "So, this looks pretty good." She made a weak gesture toward the screen.

A moment's hesitation from Dan set her pulse racing, and then he turned to the screen and nodded. "Yeah. Looks great."

"So." Scarlett stood, smiling. "Back to work." She exhaled and walked briskly back to her desk. But her heart was still pounding.

11

The following morning, Scarlett arrived at the office early, her mind still buzzing with ideas for ChronicleMe's privacy controls—and Dan. As she settled at her desk, she noticed a sticky note attached to her monitor. In Dan's messy scrawl, the note read:

Thanks for yesterday. You got me through it. -D

A warm flutter filled her chest, and she couldn't help the small smile that crept onto her face.

Her moment of contentment was short-lived as Victoria's sharp voice cut through the quiet office. "Dan, we need to talk. Now."

Scarlett peered over her cubicle and saw Victoria, impeccably dressed as always, marching toward him. Dan looked as surprised as Scarlett felt.

"Victoria, I thought I made it clear yesterday that—"

"This isn't about yesterday," Victoria interrupted, her voice low but intense. "This is about saving this project. Now, are we going to talk in private, or should I air our dirty laundry in front of the whole office?"

With a resigned sigh, Dan ushered Victoria to a meeting room and shut the door. Scarlett tried to focus on her work, but she couldn't resist glancing at the closed door every few minutes, wondering what was being said behind it.

About twenty minutes later, the door opened. Victoria emerged, looking smug, while Dan appeared frustrated but resigned. On her way past Scarlett's desk, Victoria paused.

"Team meeting in an hour," she announced, her tone indicating that she would brook no argument. "Course correction."

Scarlett's heart sank. *That can't be good.*

After an hour, the team gathered in the conference room. The atmosphere was tense, with Zoe and Diego studiously avoiding eye contact, and Dan looking like he'd rather be anywhere else.

Victoria stood at the head of the table, practically vibrating with barely contained excitement. "Ladies and gentlemen, I know yesterday was... challenging. But Dan and I have discussed it, and we agree that we need to lean into this personal angle, not shy away from it."

Scarlett's eyes widened. *You agreed? There is no way that happened—not without a firearm. Or maybe she slipped something into his latte.* Dan wouldn't meet her gaze.

Victoria continued, seeming unaware of the team's palpable tension. "The public response to Dan's story has been overwhelmingly positive. Now, people are connecting with ChronicleMe on an emotional level. We need to capitalize on that."

"Capitalize?" Scarlett couldn't hold herself back anymore. "On Dan's personal tragedy?"

Victoria's smile remained firm. "Of course, and we'll handle it with the utmost sensitivity."

"Pain for profit... in a sensitive way," Zoe muttered, just loudly enough for everyone to hear.

Victoria raised her chin and forced a smile in Zoe's direction. "I'm sorry, Zoe. I didn't realize you were a marketing expert."

Before Zoe could retort, Dan intervened. "Enough. Victoria's right. Now that it's out there, we can't ignore the public response. But," he added, looking directly at Scarlett, "we're not going to compromise our values."

Scarlett couldn't wait to see how they pulled that off.

The meeting continued, with Victoria pushing for more personal stories from the team and meeting with varying degrees of resistance. By the end, Scarlett was unconvinced but resigned to the inevitable.

As the team filed out, Scarlett hung back. "Dan, can we talk?"

He nodded, looking as tired as she felt.

Once the two of them were alone, Scarlett didn't mince words. "Are you sure about this? It feels like we're crossing a line."

Dan ran a hand through his hair. "I don't like it, but the story is out there, and Victoria made some compelling points. If sharing my story can help others, isn't that worth it?"

"Not if it hurts you. Dan, don't you think we should —" Scarlett was cut off by a knock at the door. Diego poked his head into the room.

"Sorry to interrupt, but Dan, there's a call you need to take. It's the investors."

Dan's eyes widened. "I'll be right there." He turned back to Scarlett. "We'll finish this later, okay?"

Scarlett nodded. But as he rushed out, she felt like the project was spiraling out of control.

OVER THE NEXT FEW DAYS, the office buzzed with activity. Victoria was everywhere, pushing for more personal stories and more emotional angles, demands that Scarlett managed to dodge. But her days grew increasingly long as she tried to keep up with the company's accelerating production schedule.

She and Dan were spending more time together, too, often working late into the night. Their growing closeness didn't go unnoticed by the rest of the team.

"So, you and Dan..." Zoe said one afternoon, perching on the edge of Scarlett's desk.

Scarlett felt her cheeks heat up. "Is that a question? 'Cause if it is, the answer is no."

It wasn't so much that she didn't trust Zoe—it was that Scarlett didn't know how much of what she said might filter back in some form to Diego. Despite Zoe's insistence that they were over as a couple, the tension between them was electric. Like a live wire, it could light up a room or threaten anyone who came close with its lethal voltage. Scarlett couldn't take a chance that Zoe would let something slip to him.

Zoe raised an eyebrow. "Uh-huh. All those long days and late nights of looking and longing..."

"There's no looking or longing," Scarlett protested, but even she could hear the lack of conviction in her voice.

Zoe's expression softened. "Hey, I get it. Dan's a great guy. Just... be careful, okay? I mean, look at me. This is what an office romance can do."

Scarlett nodded, grateful for her friend's concern. "Don't worry. Everything's fine."

Even as she said that, Scarlett knew it wasn't entirely true. Would she and Dan be next year's Diego and Zoe?

LATE THAT EVENING, Scarlett and Dan were in a meeting room, hunched over Dan's computer. He tilted his chair back. "That's it. I think we've finally got the privacy settings right," he said, his voice tinged with relief. "Users have complete control over what they share and with whom."

Scarlett nodded, acutely aware of how close they were sitting to each other. "It looks good."

Dan heaved a sigh. "Thanks."

"That last transition you tweaked really smoothed out the flow, and the colors highlight their options."

Dan turned and faced Scarlett, brushing his knees against hers. "Thanks."

The sincerity in his voice made her heart race. "You don't have to thank me."

"No, I mean, thanks for being here with me..."

Their eyes met, and suddenly, the air between them felt charged again. Dan's gaze dropped to her lips, and Scarlett leaned in...

"Oh! Sorry, I didn't realize anyone was still here."

They sprang apart at the sound of Victoria's voice. She stood in the doorway, a knowing smirk on her face.

"Don't let me interrupt," she said, her tone suggestive. "I was just leaving some notes on the new marketing strategy. I'll see you both tomorrow."

As Victoria's heels clicked down the hallway, Scarlett and Dan sat in awkward silence.

"I should probably go," Scarlett said as she frantically gathered her possessions.

Dan nodded, looking as flustered as she felt. "Right. Yeah. I'll, uh, I'll see you tomorrow."

Scarlett hurried out, her mind whirling. *Thanks, Victoria, for giving me yet one more reason to hate you.*

THE NEXT DAY, Scarlett couldn't help but notice the knowing looks and whispers that seemed to follow her and Dan around the office. Apparently, Victoria's mouth was prolific.

"Ignore them," Zoe advised during their lunch break. "Office gossip always dies down eventually."

Scarlett picked at her salad, her appetite gone. "Do

we have a time frame on 'eventually'? Are we talking days... a decade... post-menopause...?"

"Yes." Zoe reached across the table and squeezed Scarlett's hand. "Anyway, you and Dan are adults. You're professionals. And besides, you're so cute together!"

Before Scarlett could respond, Diego approached their table. "Hey, Zoe, can we talk?"

In an instant, Zoe's cheery expression disappeared. "I'm kind of in the middle of something."

"It'll just take a minute."

Scarlett could see the conflict on her friend's face. "It's okay," she said softly. "We can finish our chat later."

With a resigned sigh, Zoe stood up. "Fine. But make it quick."

As Zoe and Diego walked away, Scarlett wondered about the complicated history between the two. She only hoped Zoe wasn't walking toward more heartache. She deserved better.

Scarlett was so lost in thought that she didn't notice Dan's approach until he was right beside her.

"Hey," he said, his voice low. "About last night," he began, "I'm sorry."

I'm not—or I wasn't until you said that.

Scarlett forced a bright expression onto her face. "No problem," she chirped. *Big problem.*

"This whole thing—"

What thing? The app thing? The "us" thing?

"It's just... a lot to... deal with."

"I know." *You mean me? I'm a lot to deal with? 'Cause I thought I was pretty low maintenance.*

A commotion from outside interrupted the moment. They rushed out to find Zoe and Diego in the middle of a heated argument.

"I can't believe you!" Zoe said, her voice thick with emotion. "My autographed Elon Musk photo." She crouched down and began picking up pieces of broken glass and a picture frame.

Scarlett helped Zoe to her feet. "Sit down. I'll go get a broom." On the way, she paused before Diego and whispered, "I don't know what's going on here, but that photo? That was just... low."

He balked. "I didn't throw that. She did!"

Scarlett froze for a moment. "Oh." Then she turned and kept walking away but not before overhearing.

"Zoe, just let me explain—"

"I don't want to hear it!" With that, Zoe's footsteps were the last things Scarlett heard as she rounded the corner.

She returned to find Diego picking up the pieces of broken glass. "Diego, go... sit down somewhere. I've got this." Just before she turned to leave, she noticed he looked so stricken that Scarlett couldn't help feeling sorry for him.

When she was finished sweeping, she started to head Zoe's way, but Dan caught Scarlett's arm. "Give her a minute to cool off. We've got bigger problems right now."

He pointed at where Victoria was engaged in an

intense phone conversation. As they watched, she hung up, her face pale.

"Everyone, conference room, now," she called out, her usual composure shaken.

Once the team was assembled, Victoria delivered the news. "I just got off the phone with our main investor. Apparently, news of a rival app has leaked. They're threatening to pull their funding if we don't launch within the month."

The room fell into a stunned silence. Although the team had been making good progress, a month was an almost impossible deadline.

Dan was the first to recover. "Okay, let's not panic. We can do this. We'll need to pull some late nights, maybe bring in some extra help, but we'll make it happen."

As the team settled in for the long night to come, Scarlett caught Dan's eye across the table. He gave her a small smile, which he must have meant to be reassuring. It was anything but.

12

Once more, the office was already buzzing with activity when Scarlett walked in early the next morning. The rival app and the looming deadline had galvanized the team into action. Snippets of urgent conversations and tapping keyboards peppered the air as Scarlett walked to her desk.

"Morning," Dan said, appearing at her side with two cups of coffee. He handed one to her, and their fingers brushed in a way that sent a small thrill through Scarlett.

"Thanks," she murmured before taking a grateful sip. "Any news on our mysterious competitor?"

Dan's brow furrowed. "Nothing concrete yet. Max is in full combat mode, and Victoria's been working her contacts, trying to get more information. All we know for sure is that they're planning to launch in the next six weeks."

Scarlett felt her stomach drop. Six weeks? Impossible. "How did we not know about this sooner?"

"That's what I'd like to know," Victoria said from behind them. She looked impeccable as always, but Scarlett could see the strain in her eyes. "War room, five minutes."

As Victoria strode away, Scarlett and Dan shared a concerned look. "This can't be good," Scarlett muttered. "But then, nothing is anymore."

Five minutes later, the core team had assembled again. The tension was thick. Zoe sat at the opposite end of the table from Diego, squeezing her Hello Kitty stress ball with a vengeance. Diego stared dejectedly at his laptop while Dan looked weary.

A grimly expressionless Victoria stood at the head of the table. "I've managed to get some details on our competition," she began without preamble. "The company is called Cortexagon, and their app is eerily similar to ChronicleMe. They're marketing it as a 'digital time capsule' that uses AI to curate and present users' online history."

A murmur of disbelief ran through the room.

Zoe was the first to speak up. "How? That sounds way too close to be coincidental."

"Great minds think alike?" Diego muttered with a smirk.

Victoria's lips thinned. "That's what we need to figure out. If anyone on our team has been... less than discreet, we will find out."

The accusation landed hard. Scarlett felt a prickle of unease as she looked around at her colleagues. Could one of them really have leaked information about ChronicleMe?

Dan broke the tense silence by clearing his throat. "Let's not jump to conclusions. Right now, our priority needs to be getting ChronicleMe ready for launch. We can investigate the leak, if there is one, but we can't let it distract us from our goal."

Victoria nodded with apparent reluctance. "Agreed. But I want everyone to be extra-cautious from now on. No discussing the project outside of this office, no working on any Wi-Fi network but this, and of course not a word on your social media."

Once the meeting dispersed, Scarlett caught up with Zoe in the hallway. "Hey, you okay? You seemed pretty rattled in there."

Zoe sighed, running a hand through her hair. "I just can't believe this is happening. We've all worked so hard. Now it feels like it's slipping away."

Scarlett squeezed her friend's shoulder. "We can't let that happen. We've got a great team and a solid product."

Zoe tried to smile. "Yeah. Speaking of the team..." Her eyes darted to where Diego was hunched over his computer, furiously typing. "I should probably talk to him, huh? For the sake of the team."

Scarlett was torn between sympathy for her friend and the urgency of the project. "I'm not saying forgive and forget, but it would be good if you two could find a way to work together. It's a big ask, I know."

Taking a deep breath, Zoe nodded. "My brain says you're right. Let's see if I can get my heart and my temper on board." She took another deep breath and released it. "Here goes."

As Zoe approached Diego's desk, Scarlett watched long enough to see the pair calmly talking. No objects were flying, so she turned to her work. She had mock-ups to finesse and a user interface to polish. There was no time for distractions.

DAYS PASSED in a blur of activity. The office became a second home for the team, with late nights and early mornings. Takeout containers and coffee cups littered every surface.

Scarlett was in the zone, her stylus flying across her tablet. The project was coming together. She was so focused that she didn't notice Dan approaching until he touched her shoulder.

"Hey," he said softly, mindful of the late hour and the few other team members still working nearby. "How's it going?"

Scarlett blinked, suddenly aware of the stiffness of her neck. "I think I'm making progress. Want to take a look?"

Dan pulled up a chair and leaned in close to see her screen. His proximity sent a wave of warmth through Scarlett, momentarily distracting her from the task at hand.

"Wow," Dan said, his voice filled with admiration. "The way you've visualized the timeline... It's what I had in mind, only so much better."

Scarlett felt a flush of pride at his words. "Thanks. I've been trying to strike a balance between aesthetics and functionality. We want it to be beautiful without getting in the way of the user experience."

Dan nodded, his eyes still fixed on the screen. "You've nailed it."

Seeing the strain in his eyes, she asked, "How are you holding up?"

He shrugged and attempted a smile. "Me? Couldn't be better." He rolled his eyes and opened his mouth to say something, but his phone pinged with an incoming message. Dan picked up the phone and read the message, and his expression darkened.

"Is everything okay?" Scarlett asked, concern creeping into her voice.

"It's from Victoria," Dan said, his voice tight. "Cortexagon has just moved up their launch date. They're going live in three weeks."

Scarlett's stomach dropped. "Three weeks? But that means..."

"We need to push up our timeline," Dan finished for her. "We're going to have to work around the clock to make this happen."

Victoria burst into the room, her usual composure noticeably frayed again. "You got my text? Good. I'm calling an emergency team meeting. We need to strategize."

As everyone headed for the conference room, Scarlett muttered, "How? Add more hours to the day? Give up sleep? I'm pretty sure some of us have already given up showers."

When he didn't react, Scarlett leaned closer. "Dan? Are you okay?"

He turned, and the raw emotion on his face took her breath away. "No," he admitted, his voice not much louder a whisper. "Not really."

She studied that strain in his eyes, wanting nothing more than to kiss the worry away—right here in the main office corridor, before God and the security cameras. She could see the HR memo that would result from that move.

"I can't lose this, Scarlett," he murmured. "ChronicleMe... is all I have left of Mandy. If Coretexagon takes it—"

"They won't," Scarlett said fiercely. She stopped short and gripped his forearm. Realizing what she was doing, she released him and lowered her voice. "We won't let them. We're all in this, whatever it takes— this team—you, me, Zoe, Diego—maybe even Victoria."

His mouth twitched at the corner.

For a moment, the pair just looked at each other, the air between them charged with unspoken feelings, and then Dan's eyes softened. "Thanks."

Once the team had assembled, Victoria paced at the head of the table, outlining their new accelerated timeline.

"I know this is asking a lot," she said, her voice uncharacteristically gentle. "But we can't let Cortexagon ruin all that we've worked for."

The strategy meeting stretched on for hours, with tasks being assigned and timelines adjusted. By the time the group broke, the first rays of sunlight were peeking through the office windows.

IN THE DAYS THAT FOLLOWED, the office became a hive of nonstop work, with team members catching naps on couches and subsisting on coffee and takeout. Scarlett worked closely with Dan, and their personal and professional lives intertwined in ways she had never expected.

One evening, as the two were huddled over Dan's computer, reviewing the latest bug fixes, a wave of dizziness washed over Scarlett. She stumbled slightly and caught herself on the edge of the desk.

"Whoa, easy there," Dan said, concern etched on his face. He steadied her with a hand on her arm. "When was the last time you ate something? Or slept?"

Scarlett tried to think back, but the days blurred together. "I remember some pizza. And I'm pretty sure I took a nap at my desk a few hours ago."

Dan's frown deepened. "That's it. We're taking a break. Come on."

Despite her protests, Dan led her out of the office and to a small diner down the street. As they settled into a booth, Scarlett felt some of the tension leave her body.

"Thanks," she said softly, realizing how much a change of scenery helped. "There's still life out here in the world."

Dan smiled and poured her more coffee, this time from a thermal carafe. "There is. And someday we will live it." His red-rimmed eyes twinkled.

As they ate, they talked about everything but work

—their childhoods, their dreams, their fears. Scarlett found herself opening up to Dan in ways she never had before, and she felt their connection deepen with every shared story.

When they returned to the office, Scarlett felt refreshed and reenergized. Once they stepped off the elevator, they were met with a flurry of activity.

"There you are!" Zoe called out, rushing toward them. "We've got a problem. The latest build is showing major stability issues. Diego's been trying to track down the source, but..."

Dan tossed a look at Scarlett, and they dove back into work.

It was nearing dawn when Diego shouted in triumph. "I found it!" he exclaimed, drawing everyone's attention. "There was a conflict in one of the core libraries. I've patched it, and the build is stable again."

A cheer arose from the team.

Victoria stopped nervously pacing and let out a sigh. "Good work, everyone." Then her phone chimed with the sound of a message. With widening eyes, she read it. A grin bloomed on her face. "It's from our insider at Cortexagon. They're having major issues with their app, and there's talk of delaying their launch!"

Scarlett felt a surge of hope as she slowly shook her head. "It can't be."

Dan nodded, a grin spreading across his face as well. "We might just beat them to market."

They hurried off to share the news with the rest of the team.

The race was on.

13

The news of the potential delay of Cortexagon's app had injected a new surge of energy into the ChronicleMe team.

As Scarlett settled into her workstation, the office was buzzing with renewed determination. Amid it all, she caught sight of Dan in deep conversation with Victoria near the conference room. Their heads were bent close together, and Victoria's hand rested on Dan's arm in a gesture that seemed a bit too familiar for Scarlett's comfort. She tried to shake off a twinge of jealousy.

"Scarlett?" Zoe's voice broke through her thoughts. "You okay?"

Startled, Scarlett turned to Zoe. "Yeah, I'm fine. Why?"

"You look like you're trying to throw flames on Victoria with your mind."

Scarlett caught herself looking back and then tore

her gaze away from Dan and Victoria. "What? No! I'm just... thinking." She added, "About the project."

Zoe's eyebrow arched skeptically. "Uh-huh. If by 'project,' you mean Dan."

"Shh!" Scarlett glanced around to make sure no one had overheard. "It's not like that. Dan and I are... Well, you know..."

Zoe wrinkled her face. "No, not really."

Scarlett muttered, "Neither do I." She looked at Zoe's knowing expression and couldn't lie. "Okay, fine. So, there's something there, but we haven't had time to—"

"Canoodle."

Scarlett smirked. "No! Talk. There's too much going on."

Zoe frowned. "Sometimes you have to make time."

Scarlett rolled her eyes. "We will. At least I will. I'm not sure about Dan. I mean, I think... I hope..."

With more skepticism, Zoe nodded. "Wow. I've just had a vision of the future!"

"Please tell me this project works out."

"Project? No, it's a vision of you and Dan decades from now. He's leaning over your shoulder, his hands wrapped around each—"

"Zoe!"

"Walker handle! You turn—slowly because your lumbago's acting up. Your eyes meet... through your bifocals. Your lips part. Your dentures come loose."

"That's enough!"

"Apparently." Zoe smirked. "If it were me, I'd want more."

Before Scarlett could respond, Diego approached them. "Hey, Zoe, can I borrow you for a sec? I need your input on this user flow."

Zoe hesitated briefly before nodding. "Sure, I guess." After a knowing look at Scarlett, she left.

Scarlett couldn't help but notice the tentative smile that passed between the former couple. *That looks hopeful.*

Pushing all thoughts of relationships aside, Scarlett dove back into her work. Hours passed in a blur of design tweaks and user interface refinements. She was so engrossed that when Dan approached her desk, she barely noticed him.

"Hey," he said softly, startling her. "Sorry, didn't mean to scare you. I was wondering if you wanted to grab some lunch?"

Scarlett glanced at the time and was surprised to see it was already past noon. "Oh, um, sure. Just let me finish up this one thing."

Dan nodded, his eyes warm as he looked at her. "Take your time. I'll wait."

With a flutter of excitement at the prospect of spending some time alone with Dan, Scarlett saved her work and logged off her computer. As she shrugged on her coat, her hair caught on a button. Dan came to her aid and smoothed the stray strands back on her shoulder. His hand lingered there. In that short moment, their eyes met, and a surge of attraction nearly swept her away. He must have felt it, too, because his eyes darted around as if he also had to remind himself that they were in an office, surrounded by cubicles. After sharing a smile, the two of them headed for the elevator.

"Dan, there you are!" Victoria intercepted them, barely acknowledging Scarlett. "I need to discuss something with you. It's urgent."

Dan hesitated, glancing between Victoria and Scarlett. "Can it wait? We were just heading out to lunch."

Victoria's eyes narrowed slightly. "I'm afraid not. It's about the investor call this afternoon. We need to strategize."

Seeing Dan's internal conflict as he turned to her, Scarlett forced a smile. "It's okay. Go ahead. We can grab lunch another time."

"Are you sure?" Dan asked, looking genuinely disappointed. Scarlett certainly was.

Scarlett nodded, trying to ignore the triumphant gleam in Victoria's eyes. "Yeah, of course. The project comes first, right?"

As Dan and Victoria walked away, deep in conversation, Scarlett tried to quash the disappointment churning in her stomach. But she reminded herself that crunch time was upon the team, and personal feelings had to take a back seat.

Deciding she needed some air, Scarlett headed to the small courtyard outside the office building. As she stepped out into the sunlight, she spotted Zoe and Diego sitting close together on a bench, talking in low voices. Not wanting to interrupt, she turned to head back inside but not before she saw Diego reach out and take Zoe's hand.

Back at her desk, Scarlett tried to focus on her work,

but her mind kept wandering. She couldn't shake the image of Dan and Victoria's heads bent close together or the sight of Diego holding Zoe's hand. Everyone seemed to have someone, while she was left feeling alone and uncertain. That was why feelings had no place in the office—they were just a distraction. She doubled down and dug into her work.

Hours passed, and the office grew quieter as people started to head home for the night. Scarlett was just considering calling it a day when she heard raised voices coming from the conference room. Curiosity got the better of her, and she began moving closer to investigate.

Through the glass walls, she could see Dan and Victoria in what appeared to be a heated discussion. Victoria was gesturing emphatically while Dan ran his hands through his hair in frustration. Suddenly, Victoria stepped closer to Dan and placed her hand on his chest. Scarlett felt her heart drop.

Just then, Diego rounded the corner and nearly collided with Scarlett. "Whoa, sorry! I didn't see you there." He followed her gaze to the conference room. "Oh. That doesn't look good."

Scarlett tried to compose herself. "It's probably just about the project. Things are tense right now."

Diego gave her a knowing look. "Right. The project." He hesitated then said, "Listen, Scarlett, I know it's none of my business, but... be careful, okay? Dan's a great guy, but he can be pretty single-minded when it comes to work. And Victoria... Well, she knows how to get what she wants."

Before Scarlett could reply, the conference room door opened, and Dan and Victoria emerged. Again, Victoria looked smug. Meanwhile, Dan seemed distracted and troubled.

"Hey, guys. How's it going?" Diego asked, his tone deliberately casual.

Victoria shot a cold look his way. "It's time to stop using the word 'guys.' It's not gender-neutral."

Diego blinked. "Neither was trying to horizontal-mambo me in your car." While Victoria's face turned a bright red, Diego flashed his winning grin. "Anyway, I've got work to do. Later, guys—I mean comrades."

While Diego walked away, Dan moved on as though nothing had happened. "So, yeah. Just ironing out some details for the investor presentation tomorrow. Scarlett, can I talk to you for a minute?"

Scarlett nodded. Her heart raced as she followed Dan to a quiet corner of the office.

"Listen," Dan began, his voice low. "About lunch earlier... I'm sorry. I didn't mean to blow you off like that."

Scarlett forced a smile. "It's fine, really. The project's important. I get that."

Dan reached out and took her hand. "The project's important, but so are you. I was thinking maybe we could grab dinner tonight. To make up for it?"

Scarlett hesitated, the image of Victoria's hand on Dan's chest flashing through her mind. "I don't know, Dan. It's late, and we both have a lot of work to do..."

Dan's face fell. "Oh. Right, of course. Maybe another time?"

Scarlett nodded once more, not trusting herself to speak. As Dan walked away, she felt a confusing blend of emotions washing over her. Part of her wanted to call him back, to tell him about her fears and insecurities. But another part, the part that had been hurt before, restrained her.

As Scarlett gathered her possessions to leave, Zoe approached her desk. "Hey, a bunch of us are going to grab drinks at the 404 Tavern. Want to join?"

Scarlett considered the idea. Maybe a night out with friends was exactly what she needed to clear her head. "Sure, why not?"

An hour later, Scarlett was squeezed into a booth at the 404 Tavern, surrounded by her coworkers. The atmosphere was lively, with people unwinding after another intense day at the office. Dan was noticeably absent, having begged off to finish some work.

As the night wore on and the drinks flowed, Scarlett found herself relaxing for the first time in weeks. She was in the middle of a heated debate with Diego about the merits of different coding languages when she felt her phone buzz in her pocket.

After excusing herself, she stepped outside to check the message. It was from Dan: *Hey, just finished up. Still at the bar? Thought I might join you guys.*

Scarlett hesitated, her thumb hovering over the reply button. Part of her wanted to see Dan, to clear the air between them. But another part was still smarting from the events of the day.

Before she could decide, the bar door swung open,

and Zoe stumbled out, looking upset. "Scarlett? What are you doing out here?"

"Just getting some air," Scarlett replied, quickly pocketing her phone. "Are you okay?"

Zoe shook her head, tears welling in her eyes. "It's Diego. I thought... I thought things were getting better between us. But then I overheard him talking to Victoria, and..."

Scarlett pulled her friend into a hug. "Oh, Zoe. I'm so sorry. What happened?"

As Zoe recounted what she'd heard—something about Diego and Victoria working on a side project together—a fresh wave of doubt washed over Scarlett. Secrets, misunderstandings, and conflict were threatening to tear the team apart. She was at a loss to fix any of it.

Before she could find the right words to comfort Zoe, Scarlett's phone buzzed again. The screen showed another message from Dan: *On my way. See you soon.*

Looking at her tearful friend and thinking about the complications that seemed to be piling up, Scarlett made a decision. She quickly typed a reply: *Sorry, not feeling well. Headed home. See you tomorrow.*

As she pocketed her phone, ignoring the pang of guilt she felt, Scarlett turned to Zoe. "Come on, let's get out of here. We can go back to my place, open a bottle of wine, and forget about work and men for a while."

Zoe managed a watery smile. "That sounds perfect."

While starting the car, Scarlett couldn't help but feel like the situation was spiraling out of control. The launch of ChronicleMe was just weeks away, and instead of coming together as a unit, the team seemed to be fracturing under the pressure.

She thought about Dan, who was probably on his way to the bar now, and felt a mixture of longing, uncertainty, and guilt. She wanted to believe in what they'd started, but the events of the day had shaken her confidence. Moreover, they reminded her why workplace romances were never a good idea.

As she pulled away from the curb, Scarlett caught a glimpse of Dan rounding the corner on his way to the bar. For a moment, she was tempted to stop and call out to him. But he opened the door to the 404 Tavern and disappeared inside.

Scarlett focused on the road. The car ride was quiet, with Zoe sniffling occasionally beside her. Scarlett's mind raced with everything that had happened. The project, her budding relationship with Dan, the team dynamics—they all seemed to hang by a thread.

As the pair arrived at Scarlett's apartment, she made a silent vow to herself. Tomorrow, she would confront all her work and life issues head-on. As her namesake once said, tomorrow was another day— another chance to figure things out, clear the air, and get ChronicleMe back on track. But for tonight, she just needed to escape. She would be there for her friend, push aside her own troubles, and try to find some peace amid the chaos that their lives had become.

As they entered her apartment, a tangle of emotions rushed through Scarlett—uncertainty about the future, concern for her friend, and a nagging feeling that she'd just made a big mistake by pushing Dan away. She'd been impulsive, insecure, and untrusting.

She pushed those thoughts aside as she uncorked a bottle of wine. While handing Zoe a glass, Scarlett tried to muster a reassuring smile. "Here's to figuring it all out," she said, clinking her glass against Zoe's.

Zoe nodded and took a sip. "Will we ever? Figure it out, I mean?"

Scarlett fired back, "Absolutely!" She added, "I hope."

As the friends settled in for a night of commiseration and comfort, Scarlett was sure of one thing. The next day would be a turning point—for better or for worse. The only question was, would she be ready to face it?

14

S carlett woke with a pounding headache and a sense of dread. The events of the previous day came rushing back, along with the realization that she had essentially stood Dan up last night. She groaned, reaching for her phone. There were three missed calls and a text from Dan:

Hey, missed you at the bar. Hope you're feeling better. We need to talk. See you at the office.

Her stomach churned, and it wasn't just from the wine she'd shared with Zoe. She knew she had to face Dan and clear the air between them, but the thought of it filled her with anxiety. *Now, he must think I've lost interest. Or maybe he has. Worse yet, what if Victoria has gotten to him? But if Diego managed to resist her charms, surely Dan would have. Wouldn't he?*

She shook her head, trying to dispel those thoughts. She was being paranoid. Dan had chosen her, hadn't he? Or had he? A couple of kisses didn't exactly constitute an exclusive commitment. But they had sort of agreed to give their relationship a real shot—if not in words, then in implication. Or imagination. *Oh, come on, Scarlett. Grow a pair, and don't ruin this before it has a chance to begin.*

With a deep breath, Scarlett prepared for what she knew would be a challenging day. As she entered the office, she could feel the tension in the air. The launch date for ChronicleMe was looming, and everyone was on edge.

She spotted Dan at his desk, deep in conversation with Victoria. Scarlett felt a twinge of jealousy but pushed it aside. She had to trust Dan. As she approached, they both looked up.

"Scarlett," Dan said, his tone unreadable. But the look in his eyes was intense, as if he wanted to say something but couldn't.

Scarlett tried to look pleasant. "Good morning." The other two answered in kind, and then an awkward pause followed. Scarlett drew in a breath and exhaled with a cheery smile. "Well, I just thought I'd stop by." She glanced toward her cubicle. "So... duty calls." She resisted the urge to slump her way back to her desk, but as she sat, she released an unintentional "ugh."

Zoe leaned back and looked around the partition between them. "Wow, already? The day's just begun."

Scarlett smiled just as Victoria whooshed by. Scarlett glanced toward her and muttered to Zoe, "All she needs is a broom."

As the two of them giggled, Dan appeared. "Scarlett, let's go grab a coffee."

"Uh... sure." Scarlett stood, shared a meaningful glance with Zoe, and then headed toward the cafe with Dan.

Once the two of them were settled at a table, Dan leaned closer, looking concerned and frustrated. "What happened last night?"

Scarlett fidgeted with her napkin. "I'm sorry. I wasn't feeling well, and Zoe was upset about something, and I just... needed to think."

Dan's brow furrowed. "Okay." He nodded. "Okay. Do you need to think now? 'Cause the last thing I'd want to do is... keep you from thinking."

Scarlett couldn't quite read him, but whatever he was feeling—hurt or anger—it wasn't good.

She tried to reassure him. "No. I don't need to think now. I just... I don't know..." She didn't have words, and she desperately wished he did because the silence was making it worse. When she couldn't take any more, she let it spill. "Look, yesterday everything got a little over-whelming—a lot overwhelming. And I think I got over my skis with..." She fought a sick gut feeling. "With us."

Dan's mouth opened, but Scarlett held up her hand to stop him. "When I saw you with Victoria... in the conference room... it seemed like a good time to take a step back."

Dan looked up and shook his head. He started to reach for her hand, but then he looked around the cafe and withdrew it. "Scarlett, what you saw was just Victoria being Victoria."

Scarlett's stomach was churning again. "I'm sorry. You don't owe me an explanation."

Dan looked about to smile. "That's debatable. But I want you to know..." He leaned over the table and said softly, "I like you. A lot. Not Victoria. You. And if you feel like you need to step back or... whatever, I'll respect that. I won't like it because I'll miss you."

Scarlett suddenly wished they were anywhere but the company cafe because she wanted to fling her arms around him and kiss him.

Instead, she said, equally softly, "I don't want to step back." The warm look in his eyes made her heart swell. "I think all the stress around here—the project and the team dynamics just amplified my emotions until they felt like a tangled mess."

Dan's expression softened. "I get it. This is a lot to handle all at once. But Scarlett, my feelings for you are real, and I need you to trust me."

Scarlett nodded, feeling some of her anxiety melt away. "I do."

Dan's watch pinged. While he glanced at it, Scarlett smiled and said, "I'm glad we talked, but we really need to get back to work."

As the pair headed down the hall, Diego rounded a corner and practically skidded to a stop, looking frantic. "There you are. We've got a problem—a big one."

Dan's face immediately shifted to a look of concern. "What is it?"

Diego ran a hand through his hair, a gesture of frustration that reminded Scarlett of Dan. "It's the core algorithm. I was doing some final testing, and I found a major flaw. If we don't fix it, the whole app could skew all the data or even crash on launch day."

Scarlett's heart sank. They were so close to the finish line, and now this. She could see the same worry reflected in Dan's eyes.

"How bad is it?" Dan asked, his voice tight.

Diego shook his head. "Bad. We're talking about potentially exposed user data or erratic behavior in the AI... It's a mess."

Dan took a deep breath, visibly steeling himself. "Okay. Get the team together. We need all hands on deck for this one."

As Diego hurried off to gather the rest of the team, Dan turned to Scarlett. "We'll talk later."

Scarlett nodded, understanding. "Of course. What do you need me to do?"

"Start reviewing the UI. Make sure there aren't any elements that could contribute to the instability—just to cover all the angles."

With that, they both dove into crisis mode. The next few hours were a blur of frantic coding, heated discussions, and mounting frustration. Scarlett worked closely with Zoe, trying to identify any potential issues in the user interface that could be exacerbating the core problem.

As the day wore on, tensions in the office began to rise. Victoria was constantly hovering, demanding updates and reminding everyone of the looming deadline. Diego and Dan were locked in an intense debate about the best approach to fixing the algorithm, their voices occasionally rising enough for everyone to hear.

Scarlett was so focused on her work that she barely noticed when Zoe slipped away from their shared workspace. Not until she heard more raised voices did she look up and spot Zoe and Diego in a heated argument near the break room.

"I can't believe you're working with her behind our backs!" Zoe was saying, her voice thick with emotion.

Diego looked bewildered. "What are you talking about? Working with who?"

"Victoria! I heard you two talking about some side project. After everything we've been through, how could you?"

Scarlett winced, remembering Zoe's tearful confession from the night before. She wanted to intervene and support her friend, but she knew Zoe and Diego needed to work this matter out on their own.

Just then, Dan's voice cut through the tension. "Enough! We don't have time for personal drama right now. We need to focus on fixing this bug before it tanks the entire project."

The room fell silent, everyone chastened by Dan's outburst. Scarlett had never seen him lose his cool like this before, and it worried her. The stress was clearly getting to all of them.

As the team reluctantly returned to their tasks, Scarlett caught Dan's eye across the room. He looked exhausted, the weight of leadership heavy on his shoulders. She wanted to approach him and offer some words of comfort or encouragement, but Victoria beat her to it.

Scarlett watched as Victoria placed a hand on Dan's arm and leaned in close to whisper something in his ear. Whatever she said made Dan nod, his posture straightening slightly. Scarlett rolled her eyes and turned back to her work.

The hours ticked by, and progress came in fits and starts. Every time the team thought they'd found a solution, another problem would crop up. As the reality of their situation set in, the mood in the office grew increasingly grim. If they couldn't fix this bug, ChronicleMe might never see the light of day.

It was nearing midnight when Dan finally called for a break. "Everyone, take an hour. Get some food. Get some air. We'll regroup and tackle this with fresh eyes."

As the team began to disperse, Scarlett approached Dan. "Hey, how are you holding up?"

Dan ran a hand over his face, looking more vulnerable than she'd ever seen him. "Honestly? I'm terrified."

Scarlett gazed into his eyes, which were taut with stress. "Take your own advice. Take a break and come back with fresh eyes."

Dan leaned closer. "You're right. Let's go—"

Before he could finish, Victoria's voice cut through the moment.

"Dan, let's talk options. If we can't fix this in the next twenty-four hours, we need to consider postponing the launch."

His expression hardening, Dan pulled away from Scarlett. "No. We'll fix this. We have to."

Victoria stood her ground. "Fine, then explain it to me." With a nod toward the conference room, she turned and headed that way, apparently expecting Dan to follow.

Dan cast a weary look at Scarlett. With an encouraging nod, she sent him on his way. Not that she was happy about it. She cared for Dan more than ever, but something was constantly pulling them apart.

Needing some air, Scarlett headed to the roof. Once she stepped out into the cool night air, she was surprised to find Diego there, staring out at the city skyline.

"Oh, sorry," she said, turning to leave. "I didn't mean to interrupt."

Diego shook his head and patted the bench beside him. "No, it's okay. Come here. Have a seat." When Scarlett hesitated, he said, "Actually, I could use someone to talk to."

Scarlett sat down. "What's on your mind?"

Diego sighed, his usual bravado absent. "I've really screwed things up, haven't I? With the team, with Zoe... I never meant for any of this to happen."

Briefly, Scarlett studied him. "Any of what?" She considered whether to continue. "Is this about Victoria?"

Diego looked surprised by the question. "Victoria? No."

"I overheard you and Zoe," Scarlett confessed. "Something about a side project?"

"Oh, that. No, the only thing Victoria and I have been working on is a contingency plan in case we can't fix the bug in time. That's all."

"Does Zoe know that?"

Diego's shoulders slumped. "I don't think so. I

mean, I tried to tell her, but... well, I can't really blame her. I haven't exactly given her any reason to trust me."

Scarlett felt a pang of sympathy for him. "You should talk to her, Diego. Clear the air. Mainly for the two of you but also for the team."

Diego nodded, a determined expression crossing his face. "You're right. Thanks, Scarlett."

Scarlett shrugged and shook her head. She hadn't told him anything he didn't already know.

Diego stood. "And for what it's worth, you and Dan are good for each other. Don't let this project mess that up."

As Diego headed back inside, presumably to find Zoe, Scarlett remained on the roof, lost in thought. Diego was right. She and Dan were good for each other. And if they ever got to the other side of this project, she hoped they'd do something about it.

She was on her way inside when the door opened. Dan stepped out and looked surprised to see her there.

"Scarlett?"

"Hi."

"Don't go in yet."

He gestured toward the railing, and she joined him. Looking somber, he leaned his elbows on the rail and stared out at the city. "I'm scared," he admitted.

Fear was not an emotion she would have expected from Dan.

He gazed into the distance. "What if we can't fix it? What if everything we've worked for just... disappears?"

Without thinking, Scarlett reached out and put her hand over his. "That's not going to happen."

Dan's eyes dropped to their hands then back to her face. The intensity of his gaze made Scarlett's heart race.

"But you can't be sure, can you?" he asked in a voice barely above a whisper.

Scarlett took a deep breath, gathering her courage. "I'm sure that we won't let it fail."

For a moment, Dan just looked at her, an unreadable expression on his face. Then, slowly, he raised his free hand and cupped her cheek.

"Scarlett," he murmured.

The air between them seemed to crackle with electricity. Scarlett leaned into his touch, and her eyes closed as Dan's lips met hers in a soft kiss.

Dan's lips were warm and gentle, his hand sliding into her hair as he deepened the kiss. Scarlett felt as though her heart might burst from sheer joy. As they stood there, wrapped in each other's arms with the city spread out before them, Scarlett felt an uncanny peace.

He said softly, "When we get this project launched, I'd like to spend more time together."

Scarlett gazed into his eyes. "I'd like that." She kissed him, and the problems of the project and the rest of the world seemed too far away to touch them.

As they walked back inside, hand in hand, the tension that had been building all day seemed to have eased. By the break room, she spotted Zoe and Diego in deep conversation.

From her cubicle, she noticed Victoria's laser-sharp stare. For once, Scarlett didn't care. All that mattered was Dan and the soft look in his eyes when he kissed her.

Minutes later, as Scarlett settled back into her workstation, she caught Dan's eye across the room. His smile sent warmth through her chest. There was nothing that look couldn't cure.

15

The office hummed with renewed energy as the ChronicleMe team threw themselves into solving the core algorithm issue. Scarlett's fingers flew across her keyboard, her mind laser-focused on refining the user interface to complement the back-end fixes Dan and Diego were implementing.

Despite the pressure, the group had a sense of unity that hadn't been present before. The air had been cleared among several team members, and it showed in their improved collaboration.

"Scarlett," Dan called from across the room, "can you come take a look at this?"

She walked over to his workstation and leaned in close to examine his screen. The proximity sent a small thrill through her, but she pushed it aside to focus on the task at hand.

"What do you think?" Dan asked, gesturing to a new visualization of the user data flow.

Scarlett studied it for a moment. "It's good, but we

could streamline it here and here," she said, pointing at specific areas. "That would make the user experience smoother and potentially reduce the strain on the back end."

Dan nodded, a smile playing on his lips. "That's brilliant. This is why we make such a good team."

Their eyes met, and for a moment, the rest of the office faded away. Scarlett felt a warmth spread through her chest, a reminder of their rooftop conversation.

Victoria interrupted by clearing her throat behind them. "If you two are finished, we have a crisis to manage."

Feeling a flash of irritation at Victoria's tone, Scarlett straightened up. But before she could respond, Dan issued his own reply.

"We're not just managing a crisis, Victoria. We're innovating. Scarlett's insights are crucial to making ChronicleMe the best it can be."

Victoria's eyes narrowed slightly, but she nodded. "Fine."

As she walked away, Scarlett felt a surge of affection for Dan for standing up to Victoria.

The day wore on, with progress coming in fits and starts. By late afternoon, the group had made significant headway, but the core issue still eluded them.

"All right, team," Dan called out, his voice showing signs of strain. "Let's take a quick break. Fifteen minutes to recharge, then back to the salt mines."

As the team dispersed, Scarlett noticed Zoe and Diego huddled together by the coffee machine, talking in low voices. She couldn't help but smile to see them working things out.

She was about to head to the break room when she overheard Victoria talking on the phone in the hallway.

"Yes, Max, I understand the investors are concerned. But we have our best people on it, and I promised I'd keep them on schedule for you. ChronicleMe will launch on time, no matter what."

Scarlett frowned. It was so like Victoria to make promises the rest of them might not be able to keep. But what worried her most was the way Victoria had wheedled her way into a supervisory position, expanding her responsibilities beyond her original PR duties. While Scarlett could, for the most part, ignore her, she could already see Victoria claiming credit for Dan's success.

When Victoria ended the call, Scarlett approached her. "Victoria, can we talk for a minute?"

Victoria turned, her usual polished smile in place. "Of course, Scarlett. What can I do for you?"

Scarlett took a deep breath. "I couldn't help overhearing your call. I'm worried that you might be overpromising. Moving the date up was always going to be a challenge—and we are making progress, but there's no guarantee we'll solve this in time for the accelerated launch date."

Victoria's smile remained intact, but her eyes hardened. "Scarlett, I appreciate your input, but managing investor relations is my job. Your job is to make the app look pretty. So why don't you focus on that and leave the rest to me?"

Scarlett's temper flared. "This isn't about job

descriptions, Victoria. This is about the integrity of our product. If we launch before we're ready, we could be putting user data at risk."

"And if we don't launch on time, we could lose our funding, and the entire project could fall apart," Victoria snapped back. "Do you want that on your conscience? And then there's your career."

Before Scarlett could reply, Dan appeared beside them. "Is everything okay here?"

In an instant, Victoria's demeanor changed. "Of course, Dan. Scarlett and I were just discussing some concerns about the launch timeline."

Dan looked between them, his brow furrowed. "What concerns?"

Scarlett hesitated, not wanting to cause more stress for Dan. But she knew she had to be honest. "I'm worried we're pushing too hard to meet an arbitrary deadline. If we launch with bugs, it could destroy user trust in ChronicleMe before it even gets off the ground."

Dan fell quiet, evidently considering her words. Finally, he nodded. "You're right. We can't compromise on quality or security." He turned to Victoria. "But you knew that. We're still pushing for an early launch date but not at the expense of the project. I assume the investors understand that."

Victoria's eyes widened. "The investors understand that we've moved up the launch date because if they think you can't deliver, they'll lose confidence in you and the project. Do I need to explain what that could do to our funding?"

"I know exactly what it could do," Dan said, his voice firm. "But I also know what rushing a flawed product to market could do. We're not taking that risk."

Victoria rolled her eyes. "I'll pass that on to Max, but this is on you."

Scarlett and Dan watched her disappear around the corner then stared at each other in disbelief. Finally, Dan broke the silence. "Great. No pressure."

Once more, before Scarlett could respond, a shout came from across the office. "I think I've got it!" Diego called out, waving them over excitedly.

The next few hours surged with activity as the team rallied around Diego's breakthrough. Again, Scarlett and Zoe worked together closely to implement the necessary UI changes to support the new algorithm structure.

As midnight approached, Dan called everyone together. "All right, team. I think we're ready for a full test run. Scarlett, would you do the honors?"

She nodded, feeling a blend of excitement and nervousness as she initiated the test sequence. The room fell silent, everyone holding their breath as they watched the diagnostics run.

Seconds ticked by that felt like hours. And then...

"It worked!" Zoe exclaimed, breaking the tension. "Look at those metrics. It's stable!"

A cheer arose from the team. Scarlett felt tears pricking at her eyes as relief and joy washed over her. They had done it. ChronicleMe was going to launch after all.

In the midst of the celebration, Scarlett felt a hand

on her shoulder. She turned and found Dan looking at her with an expression of pure happiness.

"We did it," he said, pulling her into a hug.

Scarlett melted into his embrace, all the stress and worry of the past weeks fading away. "We did it," she echoed.

"We did," she said again, although she still couldn't quite believe it. When they pulled apart, Dan kept an arm around her waist.

Victoria looked less than thrilled, but she managed a tight smile. "Well, now that we've solved the crisis, perhaps we should all get some rest. We have a launch to prepare for, after all."

The team began to disperse, the euphoria of their success mingling with exhaustion. As Scarlett gathered her possessions, she felt a profound sense of accomplishment. Not only had they saved ChronicleMe, but she had found something she wasn't even looking for when she joined this project.

Dan approached her as she was putting on her coat. "Can I walk you out to your car?"

Scarlett smiled. "I'd like that."

As they walked out, hand in hand, Scarlett couldn't help but reflect on how much had changed. When she first joined the ChronicleMe team, she had seen it as just another project, a chance to prove herself after past disappointments. But it had become so much more.

"What are you thinking about?"

Scarlett turned to look at him. She took in his profile in the dim light. "Just about how different things are now compared to when we started."

Once they arrived at her car, Dan said, "I know." He grinned. "When you walked into that conference room, I would never have thought we'd be standing here now." He drew her into his arms and kissed her until she felt weak in the knees.

After he pulled away, Dan searched her eyes. "There is nothing I'd like more right now than to follow you home." He quickly added, "Not in a creepy way, but—you know."

Scarlett laughed. "And I might let you if we didn't have such a big day tomorrow." She stifled a yawn.

Dan raised his eyebrows. "Uh-oh. That's not a good sign. I'm boring you already."

Grinning, Scarlett shook her head. "No, that's more to do with being sleep-deprived, thanks to this project."

Dan said wryly, "Well, that's a relief." He took her face in his hands and kissed her on the forehead. "Go home. Get some sleep."

"You, too. Big day tomorrow."

He drew in air through his teeth. "Today, you mean. Launch day."

Still surprised the team had accomplished the feat, Scarlett said, "Oh, wow. It really is."

They shared one more kiss before reluctantly parting, and Scarlett felt a sense of certainty settle over her. Launch day had arrived, and with it, a new chapter in all their lives.

16

The morning of ChronicleMe's launch dawned bright and clear, a stark contrast to the frenzy inside the office. Scarlett arrived early, her stomach a knot of excitement and nerves. As she stepped off the elevator, she was greeted by the sight of her team already hard at work.

Dan looked up from his computer as she approached, and a warm smile spread across his face. "Morning," he said, standing to greet her. "Ready?"

Scarlett nodded, returning his smile. "As ready as I'll ever be. How are things looking?"

"So far, so good," Dan replied, leading her to his workstation. "We've been running final diagnostics since five a.m. Everything's holding steady."

Zoe bounded over, her usual energy amplified by the excitement of the day. "Scarlett! Thank God you're here. We need your eye on the final UI tweaks."

As Scarlett immersed herself in work, she couldn't help but marvel at how far the team had come. The office buzzed with palpable energy as everyone focused on their tasks, but underneath lay an underlying current of anticipation.

Victoria swept in around midmorning, looking impeccable as always. "All right, team," she announced, clapping her hands for attention. "The press conference is set for two p.m. Dan, I need you and Scarlett to run through your talking points one more time."

Dan nodded, catching Scarlett's eye. They had spent hours preparing for this event, crafting a presentation that would showcase ChronicleMe's features while addressing potential concerns about privacy and data security.

As she and Dan huddled in a conference room to review their notes, Scarlett felt a flutter of nerves. "Dan," she said quietly, "have we left anything out?"

Dan reached out and took her hand. "Scarlett, we've tested everything a hundred times over. We're ready."

Scarlett nodded. "You're right. We're ready." After a deep breath, she exhaled and grinned. "Everything's fine."

Their moment was interrupted by a knock at the door. Diego poked his head in, his expression uncharacteristically serious. "Guys, we might have a problem."

Scarlett felt her heart drop. "What?"

Diego entered the room and closed the door behind him. "I've been monitoring social media chatter about the launch. There's a rumor going around that ChronicleMe is just a repackaged version of Cortexagon's app, Cortexalog."

Dan's brow furrowed. "What? That's ridiculous. Where is this coming from?"

Diego shook his head. "I'm not sure, but it's gaining traction. People are questioning our integrity, suggesting we stole the idea."

Anger surged through Scarlett. After everything they'd been through and all the hard work they'd put in, to have their creation dismissed as a copy was infuriating. "We need to address this," she insisted. "We can't let a social media rumor overshadow our launch."

Dan nodded, his jaw set with determination. "We should incorporate something about it in our press conference."

Diego leveled a look of dread. "I guess someone should tell Victoria—someone above my pay grade."

Dan winced.

Scarlett said, "I'll go with you."

As she and Dan headed that way, Scarlett braced herself. Victoria had been on edge lately, with the pressure of the launch wearing on her usually unflappable demeanor.

They found Victoria in her office, deep in a phone conversation. As they entered, she held up a finger, signaling for them to wait.

"Yes, I understand your concerns," Victoria was saying, her voice tight with barely contained frustration. "But I assure you, ChronicleMe is entirely our own creation. Any similarities are purely coincidental."

Hanging up, Victoria turned to Dan and Scarlett, her expression grim. "I assume you've heard the rumors?"

Dan nodded. "We were just coming to tell you. We'll need to address it in the press conference."

Victoria sighed, rubbing her temples. "This is a disaster. The investors are panicking, and the press is sniffing around for a scandal. We need to get ahead of this and fast."

Scarlett agreed. "I have an idea. What if we do a live demonstration during the press conference? Show them firsthand how ChronicleMe works, how it's different from anything else on the market."

Dan's eyes lit up. "That's brilliant. Instead of trying to explain, we'll just show them. We could use my profile as an example, show them the depth of analysis ChronicleM*e* is capable of."

"No," Scarlett said adamantly.

Dan looked calmly at her. "It's fine. It's all out there now. Why not use it to our advantage?"

Victoria regarded him with amazement. "Now you get it. Information is our currency. And creativity comes in large bills. I'll draft a statement."

As she and Dan left Victoria happily typing away, Scarlett felt a renewed sense of purpose. They had overcome so much to get to this point. Nothing could stop them now.

The next few hours passed in a blur of activity. Scarlett and Zoe worked to prepare the live demo while Dan and Diego fine-tuned their responses to potential questions about the Cortexalog rumors.

Before the team knew it, it was time for the press conference. As they gathered backstage, Scarlett's nerves returned in full force. Dan must have sensed her anxiety because he pulled her aside, away from the bustling activity.

"Hey," he said softly, cupping her face in his hands. "No matter what happens out there, remember why we created ChronicleMe. It's more than just beating the competition or impressing investors. It's about helping people connect with their memories, with each other."

Scarlett nodded as a wave of calm washed over her. "You're right."

He leaned in and pressed a soft kiss to her forehead. "Always."

Victoria's voice interrupted their moment. "It's time. Are you ready?"

Taking a deep breath, Scarlett gave her a confident nod. "Yes, we are."

When she and Dan stepped onto the stage, Scarlett was momentarily stunned by the flashing cameras. The room was packed with journalists, tech bloggers, and industry insiders, all eager to see what ChronicleMe was all about.

Dan took the lead, his voice steady as he introduced the app and its features. Scarlett watched him with a mix of pride and admiration, marveling at how far they'd both come since their first contentious meeting.

Then came Scarlett's turn to speak, and she felt a surge of confidence. She talked about the user interface and how the team had designed ChronicleMe to be intuitive and engaging while still respecting user privacy.

As the presentation moved into the demonstration phase, Scarlett could feel the energy in the room shift.

People leaned forward in their seats, clearly intrigued by what they were seeing.

Dan walked the audience through his ChronicleMe profile, showing how the app had analyzed his social media history, photos, and personal notes to create a rich, multifaceted portrait of his life.

"As you can see," he was saying, "ChronicleMe doesn't just collect data. It finds connections, highlights patterns, and helps users see their lives in a whole new way."

Suddenly, a voice called out from the audience. "But how is this different from Cortexalog? Aren't you just copying their idea?"

Scarlett felt her heart race, but Dan remained calm. "I'm glad you asked that question," he said, his voice steady. "While it's true that both ChronicleMe and Cortexalog deal with personal data, the similarities end there. Let me show you."

He pulled up a side-by-side comparison of ChronicleMe and Cortexalog, using a slideshow Diego and Zoe had hastily cobbled together from publicly available information. As he walked the audience through the differences—ChronicleMe's advanced AI, its more robust privacy controls, and its ability to integrate a broader range of data sources—Scarlett could see the skepticism in the room start to fade.

By the time they opened the floor for questions, the mood had shifted dramatically. Instead of accusations, they were met with genuine curiosity and excitement about ChronicleMe's potential.

As the press conference wound down, Scarlett

detected Victoria from the side of the stage. She was beaming.

When, at last, the event was over, Scarlett and Dan made their way backstage, where another wave of emotion washed over her. They had done it. Against all odds, they had launched ChronicleMe, and it was a success.

The team gathered in a small room off the main stage, the air thick with a mix of exhaustion and elation.

"We did it," Zoe said, her voice filled with wonder. "We actually did it."

Grinning, Diego slung an arm around her shoulders. "Was there ever any doubt?"

Victoria cleared her throat, drawing everyone's attention. "I just got off the phone with our main investor," she said, a rare smile playing on her lips. "They're thrilled. The initial download numbers are exceeding all projections."

The team burst into a cheer. Scarlett felt tears pricking at her eyes, overwhelmed by the magnitude of what they had accomplished.

Dan pulled her into a hug, his arms strong and reassuring around her. "We did it," he murmured into her hair. "You were amazing out there."

As they broke apart, Scarlett looked around at her team—no, her friends. Zoe and Diego, their past issues seemingly resolved, stood close together, matching grins on their faces. For once, Victoria had dropped her polished facade, allowing herself to truly celebrate with the team.

"I think this calls for a celebration," Dan announced. "Drinks at the 404 Tavern, on me!"

As everyone left the conference center, Scarlett fell into step beside Dan. "I can't believe it," she said, still slightly dazed. "It's really happening."

Dan smiled, taking her hand. "Believe it. ChronicleMe is out in the world."

When they joined the others at the bar, raising a toast to ChronicleMe's successful launch, Scarlett couldn't help but reflect on the journey that had brought them here. From her initial skepticism about the project to the many obstacles they had overcome, the process had been a roller coaster of emotions and challenges.

But looking around at the team and at Dan, who had become so much more than a colleague, Scarlett knew she wouldn't change a thing. ChronicleMe had not only launched successfully but had brought them all together in ways they could never have anticipated.

As the night wore on and the celebration continued, Scarlett found a quiet moment with Dan. "So," she said, a teasing lilt to her voice, "what's next for the great Dan Weston? Now that you've revolutionized the tech world, I mean."

Dan chuckled, pulling her close. "Well, I was thinking of taking this amazing woman I know on a proper date. No work talk, no app emergencies. Just us."

Scarlett's heart skipped a beat. "If she's who I think she is, I can assure you she'd like that very much."

As they shared a soft kiss, the sounds of their

friends' laughter in the background, a sense of contentment washed over Scarlett. ChronicleMe was launched, yes, but this was just the beginning of the app's journey, of her relationship with Dan, of this new chapter in all their lives.

And Scarlett couldn't wait to see what memories they would chronicle next.

17

Much like the app's development period, the weeks following ChronicleMe's launch were intense. The app's popularity exceeded even the team's most optimistic projections, and the team found themselves working around the clock to keep up with demand and address minor bugs that inevitably cropped up.

Scarlett arrived at the office early one morning, a cup of coffee in hand and a spring in her step. Despite the long hours she was putting in, she felt energized by the app's success and the positive feedback pouring in from users.

As she settled at her desk, she found a sticky note stuck to her monitor. In Dan's now-familiar scrawl, it read:

Dinner tonight? No shop talk, I promise. -D

A smile spread across Scarlett's face. Even with their busy schedules, Dan had been true to his word about taking her on a proper date. They'd managed to sneak in a few dinners and even a weekend brunch, but this invitation felt different. More intentional.

"Someone's looking happy this morning," Zoe's voice broke through Scarlett's thoughts. "Hot date plans?"

Scarlett tried to look more neutral, but it was a lost cause. "Maybe," she admitted. "Dan left a note asking me to dinner."

Zoe's eyes lit up. "Oh, how romantic! It's about time you two had a real date. All this working late together is not the same thing, you know."

Scarlett couldn't respond before Victoria's voice rang out across the office. "Team meeting in five minutes, everyone. We have some important matters to discuss."

Exchanging curious glances, Scarlett and Zoe walked to the conference room. Dan was already there, deep in conversation with Diego. He looked up as Scarlett entered, a warm smile blooming on his face.

Once everyone was settled, Victoria cleared her throat. "First of all, I want to congratulate all of you on ChronicleMe's incredible success. The app is killing it, and it's all thanks to your hard work and dedication."

Scarlett felt Dan's hand find hers under the table and give it a gentle squeeze.

"However," Victoria continued, her tone growing serious, "with success comes new challenges. We've been receiving some concerning feedback from a small but vocal group of users."

The mood in the room shifted instantly.

"What kind of feedback?" Dan asked, leaning forward.

Victoria pulled up a series of screenshots on the large screen. "Some users are reporting that ChronicleMe is surfacing memories they'd rather forget. Painful experiences, embarrassing moments, even traumatic events they've tried to put behind them."

Scarlett's stomach dropped. This was precisely the kind of issue she'd been worried about from the beginning, but she thought they'd solved it. "Are these isolated incidents, or are we seeing a pattern?"

"It's hard to say at this point," Victoria admitted. "But it's enough to cause concern. We need to address this quickly before it escalates."

The room erupted into discussion, with everyone offering ideas and potential solutions. Scarlett found herself torn between her instinct to protect users and her belief in ChronicleMe's potential for good.

"What if we implemented a feature that allows users to preemptively hide certain memories or time periods?" she suggested. "It would give them more control over what the app surfaces."

Victoria shook her head. "We don't want the app to be negative out of the gate. It would cast a less positive light on the user experience."

Dan rubbed his forehead. "Not if we couch it in positive terms—like a quick questionnaire with some appealing graphics." He glanced at Scarlett. "Being sensitive to emotional context has to be better than surprising users with things they'd rather forget or dredging up feelings they aren't prepared for."

As the discussion continued, the growing tension between Dan and Victoria became palpable. While Dan seemed focused on finding a solution that prioritized user well-being, Victoria appeared more concerned with damage control and maintaining ChronicleMe's market position.

"We can't let a few complainers drive our business," Victoria argued. "If we overreact and start censoring content, we risk limiting the app's functionality. And that could cost us our edge over the competition."

"Some things are more important than competition," Dan shot back, his voice sharper than usual. "Like doing what's right. If we're causing people distress, we have a responsibility to fix it."

The meeting ended with a tentative plan to explore both technical and PR solutions, but the issue was far from resolved. As the group filed out of the conference room, Scarlett caught up with Dan in the hallway.

"Hey," she said softly, touching his arm. "Are you okay? That was a little intense."

Dan ran a hand through his hair. "I'm fine. It's just... This is exactly what I did not want. ChronicleMe was supposed to help people enjoy their good memories, not dredge up painful things they would rather forget."

Understanding his concern all too well, Scarlett nodded. "We'll figure it out, Dan."

"Yeah, we will. But whether Victoria follows our advice remains to be seen."

Once they returned to their desks, Scarlett dove back into her work, determined to find a solution that would protect users while preserving the essence of what made ChronicleMe unique.

The day passed in a blur of coding, design tweaks, and strategy meetings. Before Scarlett knew it, the hour was nearing seven o'clock. She was so engrossed in her work that she almost forgot about dinner until Dan appeared at her desk, coat in hand.

"Ready to get out of here?" he asked, a hint of nervousness in his voice that Scarlett found endearing.

She smiled, saving her work and shutting down her computer. "Absolutely! Where are we going?"

"It's a surprise," Dan said with a grin. "I hope you like Italian."

As the two of them left the office, Scarlett felt a flutter of excitement in her stomach. Leaving their work challenges in the office, she felt optimistic about her future with Dan.

The restaurant turned out to be a cozy little trattoria tucked away on a quiet side street. As they settled into their seats, Scarlett was struck by how different this engagement felt from their usual work dinners. There was a warmth, an intimacy to the atmosphere that made her heart race.

"This is lovely, Dan," she said, looking around appreciatively. "How did you find this place?"

A faint blush colored his cheeks. "I, uh, may have asked Zoe for some recommendations. She seems to know all the best spots in the city."

Scarlett laughed, charmed by his admission. "Well, remind me to thank her. This is perfect."

As they browsed the menu and sipped their wine,

Scarlett relaxed for the first time in weeks. Here, away from the office and the pressures of ChronicleMe, she could fully appreciate how far she and Dan had come—not just professionally but personally.

"You know," she said, setting down her glass, "when I first joined the ChronicleMe team, I never imagined we'd end up here."

Dan's eyes crinkled with amusement. "What, you mean you didn't envision yourself on a date with an insufferable tech bro?"

Scarlett laughed, fondly remembering their initial clashes. "No, I did not. But I'm glad I was wrong about you."

His expression softened, and he reached across the table and took her hand. "I'm glad you were wrong too."

The intensity in his gaze made Scarlett's breath catch. She was about to reply when Dan's phone buzzed insistently on the table. He glanced at it, his brow furrowing.

He let out an exasperated sigh. "It's Victoria," he said apologetically. "Do you mind if I...?"

Scarlett waved him off, trying to ignore the pang of disappointment. "Of course not."

As Dan stepped away to take the call, Scarlett found herself reflecting on their journey, from adversaries to colleagues to... whatever they were becoming now. The road hadn't been easy, but she wouldn't change it for anything.

Minutes later, Dan returned, looking troubled. "I'm so sorry, Scarlett, but we need to head back to the office.

There's been a development with the user-feedback issue."

Scarlett nodded, already reaching for her coat. "Of course. What's happened?"

While they hurried back to the office, Dan filled her in. A user had gone public with their story, claiming that ChronicleMe had surfaced traumatic memories of childhood abuse that they had repressed. The story was gaining traction on social media, with others coming forward with similar experiences.

When Scarlett and Dan arrived at the office, they found the rest of the team already assembled. Victoria was in full crisis-management mode, barking orders and coordinating their response.

"It's time for damage control," she was saying as Dan and Scarlett entered. "Diego, I want a full analysis of how the app is selecting and surfacing memories. Zoe, go over the code with a fine-toothed comb and figure out why the guardrails we built in aren't working. Then, the two of you fix it. Dan, oversee their progress and report back to me. Scarlett..." She paused, then, after a wave of her hand, shrugged and said, "I don't know. Add some soothing colors and whatnot." Scarlett tried not to scowl as Victoria continued. "I'll draft a CYA statement addressing user concerns and outlining our commitment to their well-being."

While Zoe and Diego, both looking stunned, left the room, Dan spoke up, his jaw set with determination again. "We need to do more than just CYA and damage control."

"Yeah, like find a way not to get sued," Victoria snapped. "Make it happen."

Scarlett and Dan exchanged a look and left the room.

For the next several hours, the team worked tirelessly to develop a solution. Scarlett worked closely with Diego to implement a new opening dialog that would allow people to "lock" specific memories or time periods, along with an extra disclaimer Victoria had drafted with the legal department. The new disclaimer contained a checkbox for users to confirm their consent and awareness of the app's potential for unexpected results.

As dawn broke, the group had formed a workable solution. Dan called the team together for one final review before they pushed the update live.

"I know we're all exhausted," he said, looking around at their tired faces, "but I want to thank you all for your hard work tonight. What we've done here isn't just a patch or a quick fix. It's a fundamental improvement to ChronicleMe that will make it safer and more valuable for our users."

A surge of pride ran through Scarlett as she looked around at her teammates. As the update went live and the first positive responses started to trickle in, the tension in the office began to dissipate.

Victoria looked more relaxed than she had in hours as she approached Dan and Scarlett. "Good work, both of you," she said, her tone grudgingly approving. "I think we've managed to turn this potential disaster into a win."

Dan nodded, but Scarlett saw the weariness in his eyes. As Victoria walked away, she turned to him. "You okay?"

He sighed and shook his head. "Yeah, I just... I can't help but feel responsible, you know? We created this thing, and it ended up hurting some people."

Scarlett reached out and took his hand. "Yes, there were unforeseen consequences. But we quickly addressed them. And, big picture, ChronicleMe is having a positive impact on the vast majority of users. That's a good thing."

A small smile tugged at the corners of his mouth. "Yeah. And then there's the matter of dinner."

Quickly, Scarlett replied, "Well, that is another matter. You owe me, so you'd better pay up—and soon." She smiled.

"It's not dinner, but I know this great little diner that serves the best pancakes in the city. I don't know about you, but I'm starving."

Her eyes lit up. "That sounds perfect." She added, "But you still owe me dinner."

Dan laughed and put his arm around Scarlett's shoulder. "Oh, wow. You drive a hard bargain, but okay. But for now, I'm thinking a western omelet and a stack of pancakes—oh, and real maple syrup—none of that artificial corn syrup crap."

As they stepped outside, the first rays of sunlight peeked over the horizon. A wave of contentment washed over Scarlett. She and Dan had created something truly special together—not just in the app itself but hope for a future together surrounded by the people they'd befriended along the way. Scarlett couldn't wait to see where it would take them next.

18

It was a clear, crisp morning when Scarlett arrived at the office, a takeout coffee in one hand and her tablet in the other. As she stepped off the elevator, an unusual sight greeted her: Dan, pacing back and forth in front of his cubicle, a phone pressed to his ear.

"No, absolutely not," he was saying, his voice tight with frustration. "We've been over this. ChronicleMe's user data is not for sale at any price."

A knot formed in Scarlett's stomach. That didn't sound good. She detected Zoe across the room and raised an eyebrow in silent question. Zoe just shrugged, looking as confused as Scarlett felt.

After a few more tense exchanges, Dan ended the call and ran a hand through his hair in exasperation. He looked up, noticing Scarlett for the first time. "Oh, hey. Good morning."

"Morning," Scarlett replied cautiously. "Everything okay?"

Dan sighed, gesturing for her to follow him into a

meeting room. Once inside, he closed the door and slumped into his chair. "That was Parana Tech. They're interested in acquiring ChronicleMe."

Once more, Scarlett's heart skipped a beat. Parana Tech was one of the most prominent players in the industry. An acquisition by them could mean big things for ChronicleMe—but it could also mean letting go of everything the team had worked so hard to build.

"What did you tell them?" she asked, trying to keep her voice neutral.

"I told them no," Dan said, looking up at her with both determination and uncertainty in his eyes. "But they're persistent. And they're offering a lot of money."

Scarlett nodded slowly, processing that information. "How much?"

Dan named a figure that made Scarlett's eyes widen. It was more money than she'd ever imagined seeing in her lifetime. "That's... a lot," she said finally.

"It is," Dan agreed. "But it's not about the money. It's about what they want to do with ChronicleMe. They don't just want the app. They want our user data, and not just for targeted advertising. They could sell it to third parties—no restrictions. It's basically everything I've stood against from the beginning."

Scarlett felt a swell of respect. This was the man she'd fallen for—someone who valued integrity over profit, who truly cared about the impact of his work.

"So, what do we do?" she asked.

Dan leaned back in his chair, looking thoughtful. "For now, we keep this between us. I don't want to worry the team until we have to. But we need to be prepared. Parana doesn't like to take no for an answer."

Just then, someone knocked on the door. Victoria poked her head in, her expression unreadable. "Sorry to interrupt, but we have a situation. The board's meeting, and they want to see us. Now."

Dan and Scarlett exchanged a worried glance. The announcement couldn't be a coincidence.

The next few hours were a blur of tense meetings and heated debates. News of Parana's offer had leaked to the board, and several members were pushing hard for the sale. Dan stood his ground, passionately defending ChronicleMe's mission and the trust their users had placed in them. Scarlett sat by his side throughout, offering support and backing up his arguments with data on user engagement and satisfaction.

As the meeting finally adjourned, the board agreed to hold off on any decisions for the present, and Scarlett and Dan were alone in the conference room.

"That was..." Scarlett began, searching for the right word.

"Intense," Dan said, a wry smile on his face.

Again, Scarlett reached for his hand and took it. "You did what you could."

"But was it enough?" They shared a moment of quiet understanding as the weight of what they faced settled over them. Then Dan straightened up, a determined look in his eye. "This isn't over. Parana won't give up easily, and we need to be ready for the next round."

Scarlett nodded, her mind already racing with

ideas. "Now that the secret is out, we should talk to the team. They deserve to know what's going on, and we could use their help brainstorming solutions."

Dan agreed, and they called an emergency team meeting. As they explained the situation to Zoe, Diego, and the others, Scarlett was struck by the emotions on their faces—concern, determination, and fierce loyalty to the app they'd all worked so hard to create.

"So, what's the plan?" Diego asked once she and Dan had finished explaining. "How do we fight this?"

Dan looked around the room, his gaze settling on each team member in turn. "We do what we do best. We innovate. We make ChronicleMe so invaluable, so unique, that selling it would be unthinkable."

Zoe winced. "But isn't that what made it so attractive to buy?"

Scarlett brightened as an idea came to her.

Seeing Scarlett's change of mood, Zoe asked, "What are you smiling about?"

"I'm being innovative." She looked around at the group's expectant faces. "What if we build in a way to protect user info—essentially blocking it from the app once a report has been generated?" Seeing her teammates' doubt and confusion, she added, "I don't know how yet, but imagine generating a report. The data goes to the user, encrypted, of course, and the data on our end is deleted—as if it were sent through a paper shredder."

Dan nodded thoughtfully. "Okay..."

Scarlett grinned. "And the best part is, if we could do that, the app would still be sellable but without any end-user data." When no one said anything, she asked timidly, "No?"

Dan brightened. "No, I love it! I'm just trying to figure out how to do it. Deleting the data is easy enough, but what if they want to replay or edit the report?"

Diego said, "If the report is converted to a video format like an MPEG, it could be edited later, but the data would all be with the user or in encrypted cloud storage."

"I like that!" Zoe said, grinning.

Diego frowned. "I do too. I just need to figure out how to protect all the data during the processing phase. I mean, we'd basically be trying to protect it from ourselves."

For the next several days, the team brainstormed, developed some solutions, and rejected others. Scarlett and Dan stole smiles across the worktable and shared too many takeout dinners with the team.

One evening, as they happened upon one another at the coffee machine, Scarlett looked over and found Dan smiling softly.

"What?" she asked, feeling suddenly self-conscious.

Dan shook his head, his smile widening. "Nothing. I was just thinking I'm glad I met you."

A warmth spread through Scarlett's chest. "Me, too," she said softly. "So why don't we just spill all the data, take the money, and run?"

Dan remained still.

"I'm kidding!" Scarlett laughed.

He also burst into laughter. "Don't think I haven't thought about it."

Scarlett sighed. "Yeah. It's like robbing a bank. Sounds fun, but it wouldn't work out the way you'd expect."

Dan quickly said, "Yeah, it would. I'd expect us to wind up in prison."

Scarlett wrinkled her face. "So it's back to plan A?"

Dan's eyes twinkled as he nodded, but he grew suddenly serious. "But I like the idea of running away with you."

"Me too."

His steady gaze sent a shiver through Scarlett. For a moment, the air between them was charged with unspoken emotion. Then Dan cleared his throat, breaking the spell. "But for now, we should, uh, probably get back to work."

Scarlett nodded, trying to ignore the flutter in her stomach. "Right. Work."

As the days passed, the team made significant progress on new features for ChronicleMe. They were in the midst of a particularly productive brainstorming session when Victoria burst into the room, her face pale.

"We have a problem," she announced without preamble. "Parana has gone public with their offer. It's all over the tech blogs."

The room erupted into chaos, everyone talking at once. In a voice that cut through the din, Dan called for quiet. "Okay, let's not panic. Victoria, what exactly are they saying?"

Victoria pulled up an article on the large screen. The headline blared, "Parana Tech in Talks to Acquire ChronicleMe: What This Means for Users."

As the team read the article, Scarlett's heart sank again. The piece portrayed ChronicleMe as a struggling startup that needed Parana's resources to reach its full potential. The article implied that the acquisition would be in the best interests of ChronicleMe's users, promising enhanced features and broader integration with other apps.

"This is a nightmare," Zoe muttered, voicing what the whole team was thinking.

Dan nodded grimly. "We need to respond. Fast."

"Already on it," Victoria said. "I'm drafting a statement refuting the implication that there's a deal in the works and further emphasizing our commitment to users. Zoe, use your social media savvy to reach out to our most vocal supporters in the tech community. We need allies in this fight."

Over the next few days, the team doubled down on their efforts to revise the app's privacy features. Scarlett was so hard at work that she almost missed the growing tension between Dan and Victoria.

That tension came to a head one afternoon, their raised voices carrying across the office.

"You can't just ignore this offer, Dan!" Victoria was saying, her frustration evident. "The board is seriously considering it, so we need to be prepared."

"I'm prepared to fight this all the way," Dan shot back. "ChronicleMe is not for sale, Victoria. Not now, not ever."

Victoria shook her head and walked away, looking troubled.

Later that evening, the office emptied, and Scarlett

finally emerged from her cubicle and searched for Dan. She stopped outside the meeting room, where she heard Dan and Victoria.

"You can't keep fighting this, Dan," Victoria was saying, her voice atypically gentle. "The board is leaning toward accepting the offer."

"Not while I hold a fifty-one percent share."

Scarlett was about to leave when the door opened, and Victoria nearly collided with her.

"Oh! Scarlett," Victoria said, recovering quickly. "I was just leaving. Have a good night."

"You, too," Scarlett said softly.

As Victoria brushed past her, Scarlett approached Dan's cubicle, finding him slumped at his desk and looking exhausted.

"Hey," she said softly. "Is everything okay?"

Dan looked up, and his expression brightened slightly at the sight of her. "Scarlett. Yeah, everything's... well, not okay, but we'll figure it out. Did you need something?"

At first, Scarlett hesitated. Should she mention what she'd overheard? But looking at Dan's tired face, she decided against it.

Dan stood up, made his way around the desk, and pulled Scarlett into a tight hug. "Are you sure you won't run away with me?" he murmured into her hair.

Scarlett melted into his embrace and said softly, "I never said I wouldn't. Just not today."

He kissed her on her forehead then worked his way, kiss by kiss, to her lips. Scarlett wished they weren't in an office, but that was the sad state of their relationship.

They were always at work, which made the idea of running away together all the more appealing.

After they pulled apart, Dan held her against him and said softly, "What if I told you I loved you?"

She looked up at him, her heart racing. It took her a few moments to speak. "I guess you'd have to tell me to find out what if."

Dan pulled away and looked deeply into her eyes. "I love you."

Scarlett couldn't breathe for a moment.

Dan's eyebrows drew together. "You don't have to say anything. I just wanted to tell you." He moved to take a step back, but Scarlett swallowed and gripped his shoulders.

"I love you too."

When Dan looked genuinely surprised and then relieved, Scarlett added, "I love you. I just wasn't expecting—"

Before she could finish, Dan kissed her once then thoroughly kissed her again. Then he laughed.

"What's so funny?" Scarlett stared at him, confused.

Dan was practically giddy, a state she'd never seen him in before. "Sorry. It's not funny. It's just—I've felt this for a while, but with everything going on here, I didn't want to complicate things. But life's too short and... there it is. I love you."

Scarlett felt as though her heart might burst. As her lips met his in a tender kiss, everything seemed to fall into place. The board and Parana could go hang. At the moment, she simply didn't care.

19

Six months after ChronicleMe's launch, Scarlett stood in front of a packed auditorium at a tech conference, her heart racing with both nerves and excitement as Dan introduced her and retreated to the wings.

"When I first joined the ChronicleMe team," she began, her voice steady, "I was skeptical. I thought it was just another gimmicky app. But what I discovered was something far more profound."

As she spoke about the app's impact, sharing stories of users reconnecting with lost memories and loved ones, she caught sight of Dan. His proud smile gave her a renewed surge of confidence.

"ChronicleMe isn't just about preserving our digital footprints," she continued. "It's about understanding the tapestry of our lives, recognizing the threads that connect us all."

After her speech, applause filled the room, and Dan made his way to her side. "Well done," he said, pulling her into a hug. "You've come a long way from the skeptic who crashed my first presentation."

Scarlett laughed, remembering that day. "We both have," she said softly.

Later that evening, as they walked hand in hand along the beach near their hotel, Dan suddenly stopped. "Scarlett," he said, his voice serious, "these past months have been the best of my life... because of you."

Scarlett's heart raced again as Dan dropped to one knee and pulled out a small box. "You helped me turn ChronicleMe into reality, and in the process, you became one of my most important memories. And I want to make more. So... will you marry me?"

Tears of joy filled Scarlett's eyes as she nodded, too overwhelmed to speak. As Dan slipped the ring on her finger, her heart felt so full of love she thought it might burst. She couldn't imagine what the future might hold for them, but she knew it would be an adventure, one they were going on together.

Back at the office a week later, Scarlett and Dan shared their news with the team. Zoe's squeal of delight could probably be heard three floors down. Diego clapped Dan on the back while Victoria offered genuinely warm congratulations.

As the impromptu celebration continued around them, Scarlett's phone buzzed with a notification. It was from ChronicleMe, highlighting a new connection in her life story. She opened the app to find a beautifully curated collection of moments with Dan, from their first contentious meeting to the proposal on the beach.

"What do you think?" Dan asked, peering over her shoulder. "I may have asked the app to put together something special."

Scarlett turned to him, her heart full once more. "It's perfect," she said softly.

As she and Dan watched the collection together, Scarlett marveled at how far they'd come. From reluctant colleagues to partners in every sense of the word, they had taken a journey filled with surprises, challenges, and, ultimately, love. And with ChronicleMe's continued success and their upcoming wedding, the future lay stretched out before them, full of promise and new memories waiting to be made. She couldn't wait to experience every moment of it, with Dan by her side and ChronicleMe there to capture it all.

20

The morning sun had barely peeked over the horizon when Scarlett arrived at the office. The past week had been a whirlwind of strategy sessions, late-night coding, and intense negotiations. Today was the day of reckoning—the board meeting that would decide ChronicleMe's fate.

As she stepped off the elevator, she found Dan already there, pacing back and forth in front of the conference room. He looked up as she approached, and his face broke into a relieved smile.

"You're here," he said, pulling her into a quick embrace. "Ready for this?"

Scarlett nodded, trying to project more confidence than she felt. "As ready as we'll ever be. Did you get any sleep last night?"

Ruefully, Dan shook his head. "Not much. I kept going over our presentation in my head."

The elevator dinged, announcing the arrival of the

rest of the team. Zoe and Diego stepped out, each looking nervous yet determined.

Victoria was the last to arrive, her usual polished demeanor slightly frayed around the edges. She nodded curtly to Dan and Scarlett before heading into the conference room to set up.

When the team gathered for a final huddle, Dan looked at each member in turn. "No matter what happens in there today, I want you all to know how proud I am of what we've accomplished. ChronicleMe isn't just an app. It's a testament to what we can achieve when we believe in something bigger than ourselves."

Scarlett felt a lump form in her throat, touched by Dan's words and the fierce determination she saw in her colleagues' eyes.

"Let's show them what ChronicleMe is really about," she added, her voice strong and clear.

With renewed resolve, she and her coworkers filed into the conference room. The board members were already seated, their faces impassive as they watched the team take their places. Scarlett couldn't help but notice a few unfamiliar faces—representatives from Parana Tech, she assumed.

Dan took his place at the head of the table, Scarlett by his side. He cleared his throat, and the room fell silent.

"Ladies and gentlemen of the board, distinguished guests," he began, his voice steady. "We're here today to discuss the future of ChronicleMe. But before we talk about offers and acquisitions, I want to remind you all of why we created this app in the first place."

He launched into their presentation, weaving together the story of ChronicleMe's inception, growth, and impact on users' lives. Scarlett watched the board members' faces, trying to gauge their reactions. Some looked intrigued, others skeptical.

As Dan finished his presentation, Scarlett stepped forward, seeing the lingering doubt in some board members' eyes.

"If I may," she said, her voice steady despite her racing heart. "ChronicleMe isn't just another app. It's a profound approach to understanding ourselves and connecting with others."

She pulled up her designs and walked the board through examples of user experiences enhanced by Scarlett's richly colored graphics and lush music. As the app experience unfolded, the board members' doubt transformed into interest then growing excitement.

"This is what sets us apart, with all due respect, from Parana or any other competitor," she concluded. "We're not just selling a product. The unique insights we offer aren't just data points—they're windows into people's lives, their most cherished memories. It's a privilege to be part of, but it's also a responsibility."

She pulled up the results of her data analysis and showed how ChronicleMe's algorithm created connections and insights that no other app could match. "We take users on an incredible journey," she concluded, "one they've entrusted us with. And that's not something we should, in good conscience, hand over to the highest bidder."

As Scarlett stepped back, she looked at Dan's face. The proud expression she found there spoke volumes.

The room was silent for a moment as the board absorbed the presentation. Then, one of the Parana representatives leaned forward. "This is all very inspiring," he said, his tone condescending. "But the fact remains that ChronicleMe needs resources to grow—resources that Parana can provide. How do you plan to compete in the long term without our backing?"

Dan looked about to respond when Victoria suddenly spoke up. "If I may," she said, standing.

Scarlett tensed, unsure of what to expect. Victoria had been acting strange lately, and there was no telling whose side she was really on.

But to Scarlett's surprise, Victoria launched into a passionate defense of ChronicleMe's independence. She outlined a robust growth strategy that involved leveraging the app's unique technology and devoted user base to carve out a distinct niche in the market.

"ChronicleMe doesn't need Parana to succeed," Victoria concluded. "In fact, I'd argue that an acquisition would stifle the very innovation that makes this app special."

Scarlett felt a surge of gratitude toward Victoria. Whatever their past differences, she clearly believed in the app as much as the rest of them.

The board members exchanged glances, clearly taken aback by the team's united front. The chairman cleared his throat. "Well, this has certainly given us a lot to think about. We'll need some time to deliberate. If you could all step out for a moment..."

As the team filed out of the conference room, a blend of hope and anxiety churned in Scarlett's stomach. They had given it their all, but whether that was enough was in the board's hands.

The team gathered in a nearby meeting room, the tension palpable. Diego paced while Zoe nervously fiddled with her phone. Dan stood by the window, his posture rigid.

Scarlett approached him and placed a gentle hand on his arm. "We did our best."

Dan turned to her, his eyes softening. "We stood up for what we believe in." He chuckled. "We might not have rent, but we'll have our principles."

Victoria joined them and took a deep breath. "I owe you both an apology. Parana approached me a few weeks ago."

Scarlett's stomach sank.

"They offered me a position if the acquisition went through. I'll admit, I was tempted. But seeing you both fight so hard for the app reminded me of why I joined this team in the first place."

Scarlett felt a wave of empathy for Victoria. Admitting that couldn't have been easy, especially given the tension between them lately.

Dan nodded thoughtfully. "Thanks for your honesty. And thank you for standing with us in there. It made a difference—to me, anyway."

Before they could say more, the door opened. The chairman's assistant poked her head in. "They're ready for you now."

The walk back to the conference room felt like the

longest of Scarlett's life. As she and her colleagues took their seats, she reached for Dan's hand under the table and squeezed it reassuringly.

The chairman cleared his throat. "After careful consideration, we've come to a decision. While Parana's offer is certainly generous, we believe that ChronicleMe's potential for growth and innovation is best served by remaining independent."

The team collectively gasped. A wave of relief and joy washed over Scarlett. They had done it—they had saved ChronicleMe.

The chairman continued, outlining some conditions —increased revenue targets and a more aggressive growth strategy. But Scarlett barely heard him. She was too busy exchanging elated glances with her teammates, feeling the weight of the past weeks rising from her shoulders.

As the meeting adjourned, the team burst into celebration. There were hugs all around, tears of joy, and promises of champagne later.

While the celebration continued around her, Scarlett took a moment to look around at the team, which felt more like a family. Zoe and Diego were locked in an enthusiastic embrace, years of tension seemingly melting away. Victoria was on the phone, already working on the company's press release. And Dan... Dan was gazing at her like she was the most precious thing in the world.

THE BAR WAS alive with the sounds of celebration. The ChronicleMe team had done it. They'd saved the company from Parana's takeover. Scarlett watched from a quiet corner as her colleagues laughed and toasted their success. Zoe and Diego were sharing a laugh at the bar, and even Victoria was smiling for once. Max sat at the end of the bar, chatting with the VP of marketing— no doubt about work.

"There you are," Dan said from behind her. "I was wondering where you'd disappeared to."

Scarlett turned, a smile spreading across her face at the sight of him. "Just taking it all in. I still can't believe it."

As a song began to play, Dan asked, with no warning, "Dance with me?" He held out his hand.

Scarlett raised an eyebrow. "Here? Now?"

Dan shrugged, a mischievous glint in his eye.

Laughing, Scarlett took his hand, allowing him to pull her into his arms. They swayed together, ignoring the curious glances from their colleagues.

"You know," Dan murmured, his lips close to her ear, "I've been thinking about the future. About what comes next for ChronicleMe..."

Scarlett's heart skipped a beat. "Oh? And what have you been thinking?"

Dan pulled back slightly, meeting her gaze. "Not just about apps or companies but life."

"Life?" Scarlett tried not to assume, but her heart raced ahead.

He smiled, brushing a strand of hair from her face. "Lives... our lives." He paused, a blank look in his eyes.

"And I'm not making any sense, am I? I should've thought about this before blurting it out."

Tears pricked at Scarlett's eyes. "Blurting what out?"

Dan ran his fingers through his hair, looking lost, before the words spilled out. "I love you." He heaved a relieved sigh. "That's all."

"I love you too," Scarlett whispered.

His eyebrows drew together as though her words couldn't be true.

"Did you hear me?" The music was loud. He might not have. She shouted just as the music stopped, "I said that I love you!" *Oh, crap, that was loud.* Scarlett looked around. Every coworker had frozen—all staring at her.

Except Dan. He was gazing at her with a ridiculous grin on his face. In an instant, she didn't care about anyone else in the room—or in the world. Then Dan's lips met hers, and they kissed, and he spun her around as applause, whistles, and cheers erupted around them.

The head of HR grabbed the mic from the DJ and tapped it. "Uh... just a friendly reminder to sign up for the mandatory sexual harassment webinar on Thursday." He stepped down amid a fresh outburst of laughter.

As another song started, Scarlett swayed in the arms of the man she loved and would marry. It was official. They had found their own happily ever after.

THANK YOU!

Thank you for reading! If you enjoyed this book, please consider leaving a review or a rating. Your feedback on bookstore, Goodreads, and Bookbub websites helps other readers discover books they'll enjoy.

THANK YOU!

Thank you for reading! If you enjoyed this book, please consider leaving a review or a rating on Amazon or your favorite bookstore. Your feedback helps other readers discover my work.

BOOK NEWS

Sign up for the J.L. Jarvis Journal for exclusive benefits, including free books, special offers, exclusive content, and updates on new releases: news.jljarvis.com

BOOK NEWS

Sign up for the J.L. Jarvis Journal for exclusive benefits, including free books, special offers, exclusive content, and updates on new releases: news.jljarvis.com

ALSO BY J.L. JARVIS

Waterfront Summers

(Can be read in any order)

The Cottage at Peregrine Cove

The House on Serenity Lake

Moonlight on Mariner's Bluff

Drake & Wilde Mysteries

(Reading Order)

1 Love in the Time of Pumpkins

2 Secrets in the Hollow

3 Shadow of the Horseman

Standalones

(Can be read in any order)

A Kiss in the Rain

App-ily Ever After

Once Upon a Winter

The Red Rose

Highland Vow

Short Stories

(Can be read in any order)

Seasons of Love: A Short Story Collection

The Eleventh-Hour Pact

A Christmas Yarn

The Farmer and the Belle

Work-Crush Balance

Cedar Creek

(Can be read in any order)

Christmas at Cedar Creek

Snowstorm at Cedar Creek

Sunlight on Cedar Creek

Pine Harbor

1 *Allison's Pine Harbor Summer*

2 *Evelyn's Pine Harbor Autumn*

3 *Lydia's Pine Harbor Christmas*

Holiday House

(Can be read in any order)

The Christmas Cabin

The Winter Lodge

The Lighthouse

The Christmas Castle

The Beach House

The Christmas Tree Inn

The Holiday Hideaway

Highland Passage

(Can be read in any order)

Highland Passage

Knight Errant

Lost Bride

Highland Soldiers

1 The Enemy

2 The Betrayal

3 The Return

4 The Wanderer

American Hearts

(Can be read in any order)

Secret Hearts

Forbidden Hearts

Runaway Hearts

For more information, visit jljarvis.com.

Get monthly book news at news.jljarvis.com.

ABOUT THE AUTHOR

J.L. Jarvis is a left-handed former opera singer/teacher/lawyer who writes books. She now lives and writes on a mountaintop in upstate New York.

jljarvis.com